Robin Scott-Elliot has been a sports journalist for 25 years with the BBC, ITV, Sunday Times, Independent and the 'i', covering every sport you can think of and a few you probably can't. In 2012 he covered the London Paralympics as the Independent's Paralympic Correspondent. He threw that all away to move home to Scotland and write, where his daughters persuaded him to write a story for them. He lives on the west coast with his wife and two children.

'A vivid and vibrant adventure celebrating difference and friendship. Thrilling and moving.'
Clare Balding

'A vividly told début,' *Fiona Noble, Bookseller, October Previews*

'A beautifully crafted début brimming with adventure - a classic in the making.' *A. M. Howell, author of The Garden of Lost Secrets*

'A truly enchanting and exceptional début with all the callings of a contemporary classic. It held my heart in its pages. Storytelling magic. *Scott Evans, The Reader Teacher and Primary School Book Club*

A thrilling adventure that sweeps you across the Russian steppe in the company of 3 bold & resourceful friends. A powerful message of courage, loyalty & diversity. This story will hold you firmly in its grasp until the final page.' *Emily Marcuccilli, School Librarian*

'A poignant and breath taking rampage of storytelling goodness. If you dare to believe then you dare to become. Full of nonstop action-adventure, humour, and friendship, it's a great historical insight into a place and time so different from the here and now.'
Mr Ripley's Enchanted Reads

'This is an enthralling, daring adventure and I loved every page. I really connected with the plight of the characters and felt such strong emotional pulls throughout.'
Erin Hamilton, Reading Advocate for ASSET Education Trust

'A really great read with magical twists and turns. The seamless blend of real and imagined is exciting. It's uplifting and champions the runaways overcoming adversity despite their differences.'
Heather Lace, Inclusive Minds Inclusion Ambassador

'A really magical book that will enchant children. I love that it's all about finding your family and that doesn't mean finding your blood or past. It's about finding the ones who take care of you and accept you and love you no matter what. It's a beautiful message.'
The Book Addicted Girl, Inclusive Minds Inclusion Ambassador

The Tzar's
Curious Runaways

Robin Scott-Elliot

Published in the UK by
Everything with Words Limited
3rd Floor, Descartes House,
8 Gate Street, London WC2A 3HP

www.everythingwithwords.com

Printed and bound in Great Britain by
Clays Ltd, Elcograf S.p.A.

A CIP catalogue record for this book is available from
the British Library.

ISBN   978–1–911427–13–1

For Karen

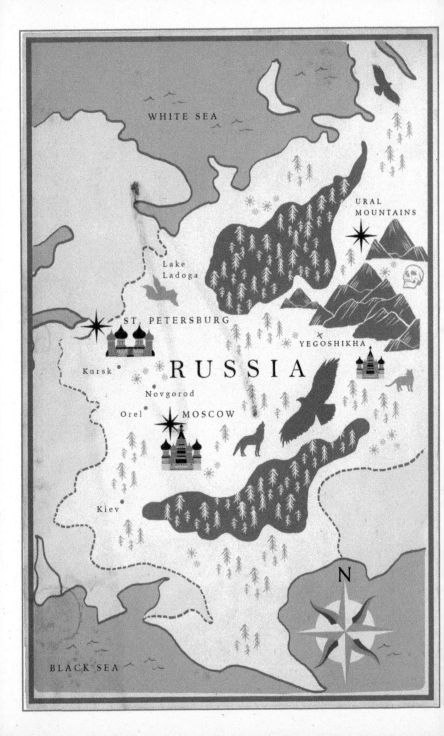

1

Katinka Dashkova wanted to live, so she held her breath. She had no choice. If she was to survive, she must be quiet as stone, as still as the statues decorating the great rooms of the Winter Palace. One ripple of the curtain behind which she crouched and he would find her.

She was trapped in a deadly game of hide and seek. The urge to open a finger-sized gap in the heavy red curtain and risk a peek out into the Tzar's private dining room tingled along her arms, heading for her fingers. She wanted to see; to see when he came into the room, to see if he really was holding a knife.

The 'game' had begun on the top floor of the Palace. Katinka, or Kat to her handful of friends, had just stepped out of the stairway that led from her sleeping quarters in the attic. The man yelled when he saw her.

"Death to the Tsar's Circus!"

Kat decided that was all she needed to hear and took flight. It always surprised people how light she was on her feet. She was used to the way people looked at her and didn't see her. Why couldn't they see her dancing feet, her blue eyes, her shiny hair, her smile as wide as the river Neva that flows past the palace and divides St Petersburg? In their twisted minds she was 'a freak' because she belonged to the Tzar's collection of people who were different. He called them my Circus of Curiosities. They came from all over his vast empire. To her friends she was Kat, to everyone else she was a person without a name. Everyone but the Tzar, Peter the Great, the all-powerful ruler of Russia, the keeper of life and the bringer of death. He called her Katinka and liked to watch her dance, usually in this room and once in front of the entire Court.

But Peter was dead – greatness doesn't make you immortal – and the Empress, the Tzarina, wanted rid of people like her.

Kat twisted her head so she could snatch a look at her pursuer, the man who wanted to kill her. Her glance revealed he was red-faced, short, fat and round. It was like being chased by a dangerous dumpling.

Where to go? Where to run to? If only she could clear her head – she was blessed with a memory that required only a single look at something to store it in her mind. That was in normal times. It was, she was discovering, rather more difficult to think straight running for your life.

In normal circumstances she knew the Palace, knew every nook and cranny. One night, when she had given up chasing sleep around her head, she tried to draw a map of every room because Kat liked to be precise about things but dawn came before she finished.

She dashed down the stairs and into the shadowy courtyard. She saw no-one, and if she shouted no-one would come to help. Who would dare defy the wishes of the Tzarina?

"I want them all gone – hunt them out," the Tzarina had declared, "remove them from every nook and cranny they have crawled into in my palace."

The noblemen of the Court turned it into a game. They liked to live in a world where people's lives meant nothing. So they decided to hunt down the living members of Peter the Great's Kunstkamera, his Circus of Curiosities.

Officially, they were to be rounded up and sent to Tzarevna Praskovia Ivanova, Peter's niece, daughter of Ivan V, a shy woman who had always found it difficult to make up her mind on anything and who now looked after the dead Tzar's human collection. She, as much anybody did, cared for them.

But if any of the Curiosities suffered an 'accident' during the round-up then these things couldn't be helped. That's what the not-so-noble nobles decided, and the Tzarina turned a blind eye because she had an Empire to rule and a throne to protect. After all accidents, as everyone knows, do happen.

On the other side of the courtyard, the door to the Tzar's quarters was open and, not stopping or caring how unusual that was, Kat darted in, raced through to the dining room and tried to make herself invisible behind the curtain.

"Ah-ahhhhhh witch – I have you!"

The curtain was ripped back and there he was and, yes, he did have a knife. Kat stared at it.

The man raised the knife but he was out of breath. Dumplings aren't designed to run. Kat seized her chance and dived between his legs. She threw herself into the curtains disguising the far door (Peter, it's said, preferred rooms to have at least two doors so there was always another way out), scrambled for the handle and plunged into the near darkness of the neighbouring room.

She lost her footing and skidded across the smooth wooden floor. She scrambled on all fours towards the far wall. The dumpling leapt in front of her, the knife glinted in the candlelight as he raised it once more.

A sudden shadow flickered across the candle mounted on the wall by the door.

"Oooooooofffffftttt," said the dumpling.

Kat looked up in time to see him stagger against the wall and slide to the floor. His knife clattered to the ground. He finished in a sitting position, head lolling forward, tongue hanging out the corner of his mouth, his many chins disappearing into his chest and large belly. She noticed how little his legs were. They looked too small to carry such a weight.

Kat let her breath out in a great sigh. She looked into the dark alcove to one side of the door, a space usually occupied by one of Peter's bodyguards.

"Have you killed him? There'll be all sorts of trouble if you have."

"He'll live."

The voice that answered was that of a boy, a teenage boy, but the figure who stepped forward into the half-light was that of a man, and a man about the height of Peter the Great himself.

"Oh, Alexei, I'm sorry – thank you."

Kat sprang to her feet and hugged him as best she could. They were the same age, 14 at their last birthday, but Alexei towered head, shoulders and chest above her.

"Saw him go after you, followed," said Alexei. He stopped talking as if that was all the explaining he needed to do. He was a boy of few words, using them carefully as though scared they might run out and he would be left with nothing to say.

Strictly speaking, Alexei wasn't part of the Kunstkamera. He was being trained as the Tzar's bodyguard. Peter the Great liked his bodyguards to be giants. Alexei's father was seven feet, two inches in his socks, and Alexei was heading the same way.

Alexei's problem was the same as Kat's – the Tzar was gone. And with the death of, to give him his full title (take a deep breath), the Most Excellent and Great Sovereign Prince Peter Alekseevich, Ruler of all Russia, Tzar of Kazan, Tzar of Astrakhan, Tzar of Siberia, Sovereign of Pskov, Great Prince of Smolensk, Tversk, Yugorsk, Permsky, Vyatsky, Bulgarsky, Sovereign of the Northern Lands, the Iverian Lands, Ruler of the Georgian Kings, of the Circassian and Mountain Princes – with his death so it seemed went their futures.

"What's happening, Alexei? What's going to happen to us?"

Alexei glanced through to the dining room. He shrugged. The dumpling groaned.

"Come," said Alexei.

"Where?" wondered Kat.

Alexei shrugged again. He had run out of words.

2

The Winter Palace was alive with hidden sounds. They could hear voices around them, shouts and yells, even screams echoing along dark corridors or muffled by closed doors. But they saw no-one. They whispered an exchange as they crept along a corridor back in the main palace – Kat did the whispering, Alexei grunted replies; a long grunt for no, a short one for yes.

A candle drew their shadows on the wall. Kat caught sight of them, the giant boy crouched over as if trying himself to become small like her.

"We must get out of the Palace, get to Tzarevna Praskovia's – we'll be safe there… won't we?"

Alexei didn't even have time to grunt a reply when the set of double doors ahead of them burst open.

They pressed themselves into the nearest alcove as a roar of laughter pounded down the corridor. Kat resisted the urge to close her eyes – fighting the fool's feeling that if you can't see them, they can't see you – and watched a cocky cluster of uniformed men emerge into the corridor.

Some wore the distinctive green coat and red sleeves of the Preobrazhensky Guards, the Tzar's own guard, swords clinking in their belts.

Kat recognised the broad figure of Count Saltykov, said to be the strongest man in the whole Empire. Peter liked to wrestle him in front of the Court and Count Saltykov was wise enough to put up a good fight and wise enough to know when to lose the good fight. The Tzar always had to win.

"Man alive," bellowed a tall guard. He had a long sharp nose. Kat thought she'd seen him at Court gatherings when she and the rest of the Kunstkamera were put on display. "He really could fly. You should've let me throw him out the window, Saltykov."

"We have the one we want – and you've had your fun," said the Count, his voice low and serious.

To Kat's relief the group turned the other way. She noticed the two men bringing up the rear were dragging something between them. No, it wasn't something, it was someone and the red pointed shoes scrapping along the wooden floor suggested the identity of their baggage. They had taken Iakim Volkov, the Royal Dwarf.

Volkov was untouchable under Peter, and made the very most of it, saying what he liked to whom he liked. He had the most vicious tongue in the whole of St Petersburg, could make a laughing stock of a man with one sentence. But as he fired off his barbs, to the delight of everyone not in his line of fire, he never gave a thought to what might happen when his protector was gone.

By the look of his slumped body, life was not going to go well for Volkov under the Tzarina. One final volley of laughter ushered the men and their prize down the corridor and out of sight.

Kat and Alexei stayed in the alcove. A groan crept out from somewhere in the room. They remained where they were, frozen with fear and indecision. Neither wanted to fall into the nobles' bloody hands and neither had a convincing idea of how to stay out of their cruel grip.

Alexei broke the spell and stepped forward. Kat overtook him and peered around the door.

"Kat... Katinka, no..." Alexei gestured for her to follow him back the way they had come. She shook her head and advanced into the room.

A long table filled its middle. Along either side chairs were overturned. The floor was a mess of broken plates and wine goblets, the dark stain of their contents puddled like spilt blood. Given the evil mood that had seized the Palace since the great Tzar breathed his last, a closer inspection may well have shown the puddles to indeed be blood. But there was no way Kat was going to take a closer look.

Instead her attention was focussed on the source of the groans. They'd been replaced by a series of whimpers coming from beneath the far end of the table.

Kat crouched down and looked underneath.

"Are you all right?"

The reply was one more whimper. It sounded, thought Kat, like a puppy that had lost its mother.

"Kat... come."

Alexei filled the doorway beckoning urgently at her.

"We must get out."

"Wait," said Kat and advanced down the table.

"Go away."

"No," said Kat.

"Yes," rumbled Alexei.

"Go away," repeated the source of the whimpers.

"We want to help you," suggested Kat.

"No we don't," said Alexei.

"I don't want your help."

"See," said Alexei.

"I recognise your voice," said Kat as she reached the end of the table and stood over the whimperer.

He was curled into a ball, head in his hands. There were cuts on his hands

"I don't recognise yours – go away."

"You sing the songs."

"So do the blackbirds."

"No," said Kat crossly and aimed a gentle kick at the human ball.

"Oww," he said and rolled away like a startled hedgehog. Once he felt at a safe distance, he uncurled himself and sat up.

"What did you do that for?"

"Sorry – I'm really sorry, I wasn't thinking."

She cursed her quick temper – it was always getting her into trouble. Sometimes she needed to think first, act second.

"Let me help you."

Kat stretched out a hand, as if trying to attract a wary dog. Now she could see him more clearly, she could see the reason for every groan and whimper. His face was black and blue, blood trickled from his nose which was itself pointing at an odd angle. He held his left arm across his chest scowling at her.

"I do recognise you," said Kat, "you sing at the weddings, the dwarf weddings and in the Court… for the Tzar. One night you sang and I danced… remember?"

"No."

Kat looked around the room, saw what she was after and gathered it together on the table. She restored one of the chairs to its proper position.

"Here," she said and pointed at the chair. "Alexei – keep watch. I'm going to patch him up."

She tore up one of the large napkins the noble women used to cover their dresses so no food or wine stained them during banquets – Russian men were messy eaters and prone to hurling the odd piece of food to emphasise a point. Being hit by a flying piece of roast bear left a nasty mark.

Kat sang to herself as she wiped a bowl and filled it with water.

"Come," she said and this time the dwarf – he was one of the hundred or so Tzar Peter kept at court – stood up. He clambered awkwardly into the chair, clutching his arm and grimacing.

"Is it very sore?" said Kat in what she hoped was her best nurse voice. She felt guilty because she couldn't remember his name. Especially as she could remember every last detail of the night she'd danced before the Court.

3

There had been a banquet, 71 courses (Kat counted them); every dish you could imagine and plenty you couldn't. The centrepiece was a whole roast bear with a whole roast swan coming out of its mouth. In turn the swan had a large baked pike caught in its beak. It drew roars of applause from the Tzar's Jolly Company, as he called his court.

Peter liked to play tricks on his Jolly Company. The great tables were laid with one chair fewer than the number of guests and so the last two to the table would have to fight for the final seat to roars of encouragement from the Tzar. The loser was made to go and eat at the dwarves' table, hunched on a chair and a target for any bored nobleman who fancied hurling his uneaten bear's ear across the room.

Never trust the Tzar's soup, they said. He had a dead mouse placed at the bottom of one of the bowls. But woe betide the man who didn't finish his bowl, drain the last drop and lick his lips in appreciation.

Anyone who cried out or gave any sign of disgust would be handed the Eagle Goblet, a large cup filled to the brim with plum brandy. It must, commanded the Tzar, be drained. And once it was drained that would be the end of the night for the poor drinker – only a giant could stomach a goblet of Peter the Great's plum brandy. And often Peter would command a giant to do just that in order to prove the point.

That was when he was in a good mood. In a bad mood, instead of handing the mouse-bowl victim the goblet he would yell at their ingratitude. Before bringing the one-sided conversation to an end with a meaty punch. That too meant the end of the night for the man on the receiving end.

It was a dangerous and cruel court. For making a joke about the Tzar any courtier could have their tongue torn out by Pyotr Tolstoy, the Tzar's torturer. He was better known as The Terror, a nickname no-one ever had to explain.

But it was also a magnificent court. The women,

the Princesses, Countesses, Duchesses, dressed in great ball gowns dripping with jewellery. The Tzarina sat beside Peter, her hair piled on top of her head and glittering with gold and diamonds. The men wore the finest coats money could buy, their chests covered with golden medals handed out by the Tzar for whatever took his fancy – a fine dancer and a notable general might be rewarded on the same night.

A wise woman said of Peter that he was "very, very good and very, very bad." Often at the same time.

Once the banquet was done, the tables were cleared away and the Circus of Curiosities paraded into the room. Kat walked beside Garbuchka the Hunchback, an old woman said to tell the future with remarkable success. In front of them came Tall Daryushka the Handless alongside Beznioka the Legless Mama in a wooden wheeled chair, her baby gurgling on her lap*.

There were giants dressed as soldiers, huge axes over their shoulders, jesters from France, Rome, England and Spain cavorting and cackling, proud Kalmyks from distant Siberia in the extreme east of the Empire, tall, elegant Nubian women bought from

* This really happened at the court of Peter the Great

23

Africa by slave traders, men so fat they carried their bellies before them in wheelbarrows and then the dwarves, 100 or so all dressed in whatever the theme of the night was.

That night they were costumed as ballet dancers and ordered to dance and pirouette into the room. Some of the older ones fell as they attempted to spin, crashing into others in the parade and sending them tumbling too.

The Jolly Company laughed at them. It was cruel laughter, fun at someone else's expense. Kat closed her eyes and trusted her feet to lead her. She wished she could close her mind and imagine herself somewhere else; like her home village in the foothills of the distant Ural Mountains, playing on a sunny day in one of the ice-cold streams that danced down the hillsides.

The thud of Peter's huge cane snapped Kat back into the Summer Ballroom. The room fell silent. Peter pointed his cane and the dwarf orchestra hurried forward and prepared to play. A young dwarf, wearing a scarlet coat with gold piping and golden tights and shoes, clambered onto one of the tables.

A murmur swept the room as he began to sing. He

was small but his voice was big, and sweet and strong. Kat felt it lift her, as if she had wings and could fly from Court and land on one of the great stages in Paris, the home of ballet, where she would dance and dance and dance until her feet ached and her heart sang.

She looked towards Peter, who raised his cane and pointed it at her. Kat stepped forward. She felt the eyes of the Court on her, could sense them boring into her back. She felt a surge of anger course through her veins; she would make Them see Her, she would make Them marvel at Her.

She spun into the centre of the room, the dwarf's voice filled her head, her legs and she felt it lift them, first her right, then her left. She was on her toes, spinning, stepping, leaping, twirling, turning, dancing as she'd never danced before. Her head spun. It was the greatest moment of her life.

But like so much in Peter's Russia, the very best came alongside the very worst. The very, very good with the very, very bad. There was another thud of the mighty cane. Kat stopped. Peter pointed his cane across the room at a couple standing arm-in-arm. They were tall and handsome, a fairy-story Prince and

Princess, each wearing dazzling golden outfits that demanded attention.

The crowd cleared from around them like waves retreating down a beach.

"Prince Sikorsky," said Peter, a teasing smile playing across his face, "you are the most splendidly dressed man in our Jolly Company so you shall dance with Katinka.

"And you Princess Sophie, you shall dance with Volkov."

A titter sniggered around the room. Volkov, wearing his favourite red pointed slippers, hooted and jumped down from the table he'd been standing on. He hurried across the dance floor and bowed low before Princess Sophie. She looked away. He raised a hand towards her.

"Play, sing," boomed Peter, "and dance."

The orchestra struck up a slow beat and the singing dwarf began the opening verse of the Court's favourite love ballad.

"His arms were strong, thick as the Russian oak, her arms were as slim as the silver birch... he took her in his..."

Kat bowed her head. This must have been planned,

the orchestra knew what to play. A plan to humiliate the preening Prince by making him dance with her. Her triumph was swept aside, her magic feet weighed down by the giggles of the Court women.

She would never, she realised as she felt the Prince's arms take hers, be anything more than a figure of fun. She could feel how loath he was to touch her, feel him recoiling from her. She glanced up into his face and their eyes met. Just for a moment, but enough for her to see the hate poisoning his. It was not hate for Peter – nobody dared hate the Tzar, fearing he would find out somehow and their punishment would be a dance in the arms of The Terror. It was hate for her, and who she was.

Prince Sikorsky was to have his revenge, as he thought it, some weeks later when he had Kat whipped over some made-up complaint. She protested her innocence but who would believe her word above that of a prince. Afterwards Old Granny Garbuchka clucked sympathetically as she rubbed one of her lotions into the scars. The marks remained, criss-crossed on her back.

They danced like two stone statues. The laughter spread around the Court. Next to them Volkov was doing his duty, doing what he needed to stay out of The Terror's grip. He was playing the clown, humiliating Princess Sophie, treading on her toes then pretending she had stepped on his by hopping away howling in pain.

From his throne Peter the Great watched. The smile had gone, eyes narrowed and unreadable, and all the while the dwarf sang on, the most beautiful voice in all Russia, the voice of an angel in an age of living devils.

4

"Owww... watch what you're doing."

"Oh... sorry."

Kat shook her head, hurrying her mind away from the past. 'What's gone is gone,' Granny Garbuchka used to tell her, 'look only forwards.'

She still couldn't remember his name.

"Can you bend your arm?" she wondered.

He grimaced as she gently fixed it across his chest and used the napkin to fashion a sling which she tied around his neck.

"Fat lot of good that's going to do," said the dwarf and spat ferociously on the floor.

"Charming," said Kat. She dipped the corner of another napkin in the water and dabbed at his face. They sat in silence as she wiped the blood away.

"Thank you," he said after a while.

"Oh," she said. Thanks were rarely offered in the Court of the Tzar.

"What's your name?"

"You don't know, do you?" sneered the dwarf, as if his thanks had been a grave error.

"Well," said Kat, cheeks flushing as her temper flared. "I wouldn't be asking otherwise, would I?"

"Hurry up, you two," hissed Alexei. "We've to get out of here."

They ignored him, preferring to glare at each other. The dwarf blinked first.

"I thought everyone knew, especially someone like you."

"I'm not like you."

"Oh yes, of course. I'm humbly sorry, beautiful princess of the Court of Peter the Great, Emperor of All Russia."

Kat stood up.

"Coming, Alexei."

"No… wait…"

"Why?"

"We're the same, you, me... him." The dwarf raised his good hand and pointed at Alexei. "We're freaks, always have been, always will be in their eyes."

"Don't use that word," said Kat.

"Why not? That's their word. I've heard it enough times – damn them! And so have you. That's why you're here, that's why they took you from whatever miserable corner of the Empire they found you in. Probably sold by your peasant parents, they'd do anything for money that sort..."

That was as far as the rant went because Kat ran back from the door and pushed him as hard as she could, hard enough to tilt the chair onto its back legs, where it paused for a moment before crashing to the ground.

The dwarf squealed as he was flung from the chair and his arm hit the floor. Alexei guffawed and then there was silence. A cry rose from somewhere in the Winter Palace. It was impossible to tell whether it was one of anger or happiness.

"They never sold me... they loved me..."

"I don't have a name..."

They had spoken at the same time. The dwarf

rolled over and got to his feet, avoiding putting any pressure on his injured arm. Kat was pleased to see the makeshift sling remained in place.

"None of us do, apart from Volkov. Only the Royal Dwarf is allowed a name. The rest of us…" His voice was deeper than she expected, rougher, nothing like his singing voice. He shrugged and spat again. "Oh… sorry," he said. "The Tzar likes us to – makes us look like little barbarians, he says – it's what people expect. Important to meet people's expectations here, he says…"

"You don't have a name? Everyone has a name."

"I don't."

"But you had a name at the banquet."

"Sure I did – Cantona. They give us a name for each event. I've been all sorts. Once I was crowned as Stephen the Small by Tzarevna Praskovia and married to one of those giant women from Finland, Princess Tarakanova they decided she would be called – Princess of the Cockroaches."

"Urgh," said Kat.

"We're their toys. They play with us till we break… then they get a new one."

He started counting his fingers. "Tall Paul

Pavlov – one of their jokes. Shrimp – that was for an ocean ball, bit obvious I thought. King Charles of Sweden, that was a war scene – they fired me from a canon, a fake canon – some soldiers held me, shouted bang and tossed me into a net. Nikolai, Prince of the Cossacks… I liked that one, got to ride this little pony, galloped around the Summer Ballroom waving a sword over my head, actually cut one of the real Princes – Tzar laughed so much he was sick."

"Well, Nikolai it will be then."

"Eh?"

"Your name – you need a name, everybody needs a name and you shall be Nikolai to us. Prince Nikolai if you'd like."

"Nah," said Nikolai, shaking his head, "can't stand princes. Just plain old Nikolai will do."

They looked at each other and smiled.

"Nikolai," he said as if testing his new name. "Nik-o-lai, Ni-ko-l-ai, Nikolai."

"That's Alexei, I'm Katinka, but my friends call me Kat – you can call me Kat."

"Come ON – if you don't come now I'm going," said Alexei. He peered out the door. "All clear."

"You coming?"

"Where?" said Nikolai.

"Anywhere but here."

"Yes," said Nikolai, "yes, Kat."

5

If Kat and Nikolai, at this precise point of their lives, had been offered the chance to become giants they would probably have taken it – in fact certainly taken it in Nikolai's case. But the air is not always sweeter the higher you climb. Alexei may have been able to look down on the world but he felt trapped by what he was just the same as Kat and Nikolai.

People treated him like one of the bears snatched from Russia's great forests and brought to Court in chains. The bears were teased, poked and prodded and when they roared and swung huge paws in furious frustration they were whipped or had the dogs set on them. Bear baiting it was called. Sometimes, if there was not a bear in sight, the nobles would bait a giant instead.

Alexei had the protection of Tzar Peter but that was not always enough to spare him. The Tzar liked to see his reaction, see how many of the nobles he could bash before the Guards restrained him and put him in chains for an hour or two.

That was not Alexei's biggest problem. He could take a beating, he could take pretty much anything, just so long as he had his four meals a day. If he didn't eat, the strength drained from him. It was why his best friends, apart from Kat, were to be found in the kitchens.

The three of them headed for the Palace's main kitchen, three vast rooms around the Back Courtyard, always boiling hot, always bubbling with shouts, commands and the rough songs of the cooks as they toiled over vast cauldrons and ovens.

In the courtyard three large tables were lined up, ropes rising from them into the night sky. The tables would soon be filled with food, huge plates secured into grooved spaces cut into the table surface. When a table was covered and barely a glimpse of its scratched surface was visible, it would be hoisted up and swung into the royal quarters through large windows on the floors above.

It was the Tzar's idea. He didn't want any servants overhearing his thoughts or plans. Like every Russian ruler, Peter was terrified of plots against him.

Not that any of that bothered Alexei. What bothered Alexei was they'd got their timings wrong. The trick was to arrive when the tables were being lowered and the leftovers were easy pickings for anyone loitering in the courtyard.

The three of them hurried through the kitchen – where work carried on at its normal furious pace, no matter the horror stories playing out elsewhere in the Palace – and into the welcome darkness of the courtyard.

"Stoi."

A voice of authority rang out of the dark, followed by its owner stepping into the light. He wore the familiar uniform of the Guards, one hand resting on his sword, ready to draw and fight to the death to protect whoever sat on Russia's throne.

"Ah," he said. "Little Bear."

"Captain," replied Alexei, snapping to attention and directing a salute at the man.

"Ach, you've promoted me, you big, dumb oaf."

The man's smile betrayed the lack of seriousness in his words. "You forget, I'm a mere Sergeant."

Alexei smiled back. Flattery never fails with a man in uniform. Make them think they're better than they are, and more importantly make them think they're better than you. Sometimes it was too easy. People believed, whether rich or poor, clever or dumb, that because you're a giant you are slow and stupid. The same attitude was applied to the Curiosities of Peter's Kunstkamera – if you look different to us then you can't have a brain like us. That's what most thought, and Alexei had long since learned to use it to his advantage.

He actually liked Sergeant Zhukov, a short, square man with an extravagant moustache that curled impressively at either end and a voice loud enough to shake windows. Zhukov was a champion wrestler and had decided, having no children of his own, to teach Alexei to follow in his wrestling footsteps.

"Hungry again, m'boy?"

Alexei nodded. Zhukov cast an eye over Kat and Nikolai.

"You want to be careful who you mix with… these are uncertain times, dangerous times."

"They're my friends," said Alexei and stepped in front of them.

"You don't have to worry about me, just saying be careful, that's all."

"We need to get out – will you help us?"

Kat had stepped out from behind Alexei to ask her question. Alexei raised a hand as if to stop her then dropped it. He'd watched Kat over the last few years as she'd grown up in Court and marvelled at her confidence. He wished he could be more like this slip of a girl, strong-willed and determined.

Once, he'd asked about her back – 'affliction' was the word he used – and she'd slapped him. He was sitting, she was standing on a chair – she'd been demonstrating her twirl in a new dress for that evening's banquet. His cheek glowed and stung.

"Everything's part of me," she said, scowling at him. "I have no afflictions. If I am to be loved, I will be loved for all of me."

Nikolai remained in Alexei's shadow. He'd had enough of being on the receiving end for one day. His arm throbbed in its sling, his head ached. A low rumble caused him to glance skywards before he realised it was coming from Alexei's stomach.

"Please," added Kat. "We must get to Tzarevna Praskovia's palace."

Sergeant Zhukov shook his head. Kat tried again.

"If we stay here… I think, well… tomorrow might never come for us."

"No," he said.

Kat's stomach sank. Alexei's rumbled again. The hungrier he became, the more difficult it was to think.

"You will not be safe at the Tzarevna's palace. Maybe for a night or two but the Tzarina, she wants you gone, all your sorts, gone from Petersburg."

"Where must we go?"

Zhukov shrugged. "She cares not whether your new homes are above or below the ground – there are plenty who want to see you all below ground."

"Below ground?" Alexei looked puzzled. His head felt hollow. 'Grrrrrrrr,' protested his equally empty stomach.

"In the ground… dead," said Kat. "They'll kill us, if they can."

Zhukov nodded and looked at the ground, too ashamed to meet their eyes.

"You're a good man, aren't you Sergeant," suggested Kat. She watched him carefully. There were good men, and women, in the Palace – they were just hard to find. Her instincts were to trust nobody. That's what happens when you are taken from your parents aged six, screaming at the pain of separation. She remembered the pain – no-one hurt her, the man who took her and bundled her into a cart was rough but his hands caused no damage. Yet still there was pain, so much pain and it came from inside her.

That was eight years ago, which was 2,920 days. That was not the precise number of days she'd been away from home, because she didn't know what day she was taken. And that annoyed her. She knew it was summer – she arrived in St Petersburg during the White Nights when darkness never visits the city – but she couldn't be certain, and she liked to be certain.

As for the pain. It went away. Most of it. There was still a part of her, somewhere deep, deep inside, that ached. But she learned to live with that.

"We need a good man," said Kat, her eyes still fixed on the Sergeant.

"Dunno about that," he said. Kat kept silent and kept her gaze on Zhukov – it was a trick she'd learnt. Silences make people nervous so they say things

41

without thinking, hurrying out words to fill the silence.

"I will do what I can – probably won't be much but, yes, I'll help."

N

6

Kat was used to being locked up. The Kunstkamera were often shut in their sleeping quarters for a whole day or more. During church festivals they were always locked up. Nobody, Old Granny Garbuchka said with that air she has of knowing best about everything, wants to have to look at a Curiosity while they say their prayers.

But the sound of Zhukov turning the key in the storeroom door, the clunk of the lock slapping into place, sent a shiver down Kat's aching spine. He told them he was going to lock them in – they'd be safer that way. Even so, it meant they were now relying on Zhukov, and Kat didn't like having to rely on anyone. It was best to look out for yourself in this Palace.

"He's a good man," said Alexei, as if sensing Kat's

unease. His words squeezed out around a mouthful of cold swan. Alexei's favourite cook had filled a bowl for each of them to take to the storeroom. It was next to the guardroom and full of dusty trunks that looked as if they'd remained shut tight since long before Peter became great. They were to spend the night here – Zhukov would return in the morning.

So, Kat thought, they had a few hours to plan their future. The three of them – she'd decided three was better than one to mount a successful escape from the Palace. She trusted Alexei, and liked him. Not that she'd tell him that. He was okay – for a boy. And having a giant as a friend could be useful, as he'd already shown by flattening the Angry Dumpling man.

Nikolai she was less sure about. A singing dwarf would not be as useful in an escape plan as a tough giant, but there was something in Kat's head telling her they should stick together.

She looked over at Nikolai, sitting on a chest in the corner, chewing on a chunk of meat from his bowl. He smiled at her.

"Life's good, eh Kat? Food and a roof over our heads." He winked and then made to spit before catching himself and turning it into a cough. Kat grinned. Yes, they should definitely stick together.

She handed her bowl to Alexei. "You have it, you need it," she said.

While the boys chewed on, Kat examined the chest she'd been sitting on. She tested the lid. It opened to reveal layer upon layer of furs. They must have been gifted to the Tzar on one of his journeys around his vast Empire.

Kat lifted one out. A memory leapt into her mind, a hunter, covered from head to foot in fur, trudging through the winter's first snow dusted over a village, his sleigh piled high with furs and animal skins from a long summer in the mountains. Now with the snow arriving he was heading to winter quarters, trading his work on the way – he wanted grain, dried meat, maybe a chicken to lay him eggs, supplies to get him through the winter.

Kat blinked. The memory was strong. Where had it come from? Home. It must be home. She would have glimpsed it as a little girl, sitting in the wooden window seat of her parents' hut. The hunter must have come down from the Urals.

Home… that was it. Home – they would go home.

She would take Alexei and Nikolai to her home. The village where she'd spent the first six years of her life. She'd been happy then. Hadn't she? Her memory told her so, but when she tried extra hard to remember life in the village the picture blurred around the edges.

She could see the hut, sometimes even a big house with a blue onion dome on top of a tower, and she could see the faces of her mother and father. Everything else remained just out of her mind's reach, no matter how much she concentrated.

Kat guessed it was because she'd been little when she was taken away. Now she could go back, take Alexei and Nikolai. They could take over one of the empty huts in the village, maybe even become hunters themselves, spend summer in the mountains where the streams ran clear and the air was sweet.

"What?" said Alexei when she told them.

"Why?" said Nikolai.

"How?" said Alexei.

"Never," said Nikolai.

"Impossible," said Alexei.

"D'you even know where the Urals are?" asked Nikolai.

"Yes," said Kat. She felt hurt by their dismissive response, anger began to bubble in her stomach.

"Well, how do we get there then?" said Nikolai and laughed dismissively as he returned attention to his bowl.

Kat leapt across the room. Nikolai panicked, slipped as he tried to get to his feet and tumbled off the trunk followed by his bowl. He landed on the floor and the bowl landed on his head, the contents spilling down his hair and face.

Kat picked the bowl off his head. He was crowned by a chunk of bear meat. A dribble of gravy ran down one cheek.

"You follow the sun and the stars," she said, when she should have been following Nikolai's movement. He jerked his body forwards, wrapped his legs around one of her ankles. Before she knew it she was following him to the floor. The bowl took flight once again and this time it landed, with a dull thud, on Kat's head.

"Owww," she said, rubbing the sore spot.

"Seeing stars?" said Nikolai and leapt back onto the trunk. He was quick, nimble on his feet. He was also still hungry so he pulled the piece of meat from his head, where it had remained stuck in his thick, dark curly hair, and popped it into his mouth.

Kat lay looking up at the ceiling. Dust dropped like tiny snowflakes as footsteps marched across the room above. These furs would come in handy – winter was coming and winter was Russia's biggest killer despite the best efforts of the Tzar, his wife and the blood-thirsty noblemen.

"If we stay here we'll die."

"If we follow your plan, we'll die," said Nikolai.

Kat sat up. "Better to die trying to change our lives than waiting for them to be ended."

"Listen to her…" Nikolai flicked his head in Kat's direction as he spoke to Alexei… "… our very own freak philosopher. Next she'll be telling us it's better to die as a wolf than be slaughtered like a sheep. She's been spending too long with Old Granny Garbuchka."

Kat ignored him. "In the morning we'll go and find Johann Daniel – he'll help us; he'll know how we can get there."

"Who?"

Kat paid no attention to Nikolai, her head too full of ideas and thoughts and plans and dreams to take in anything else.

Alexei answered for her. "The strange Frenchman, the one with the pointy teeth – Johann Daniel Schumacher, the Tzar's librarian, never leaves the library. He's a soft spot for Kat."

"The vampire? They say you should stuff your pockets full of garlic and crosses before going anywhere near him."

"What?" Kat was back with them.

"He sucks your blood, that's what they say."

"Huh! Them again, what do they know? They're scared of him because he's clever, the cleverest man in all Russia."

7

The cleverest man in all Russia was stuck. He'd reached the book he'd been searching most of the night for, but in his haste to get hold of it, he slipped and pushed the ladder away. It scuttled off on its wheels – his invention to move the ladder around more easily – and stopped out of reach.

"Ah," said Johann Daniel Schumacher, his black cloak settling around him again after flapping in surprise at his slip. He held the book tight in one hand and sucked at his teeth. There was no way he was going to let go of it. Nothing was more important than his books. With his other hand he clutched the shelf. His toes edged onto the narrow shelf below so he was safe from falling. For the time being.

Johann Daniel Schumacher was not a strong man. In due course, as he was well aware, he would lose his grip and fall. When he did he would surely break something – at best an ankle, at worst his head. This could be the end, thought Johann Daniel. And as he hung there he contented himself that at least he'd lived a life – escaped his dreary home and seen some of what the world had to offer.

Home was a small town on the edge of France, somewhere and nowhere, a place where nothing much ever happened. So he had gone to Paris to find something and there Peter the Great had found him. Come and build me a library the envy of the world, said Peter and nobody said no to Peter the Great. Johann Daniel came to St Petersburg and did what Peter commanded. He loved his books (he liked to think of them as his). Now it looked as if he might die in his books – he'd reached the end of his shelf life. Johann Daniel tittered at his joke.

He wasn't worried about dying. Everyone had to die and in Peter the Great's Russia it was better to be ready for death. He closed his eyes, raised the book to his nose and inhaled the smell of its pages. He just wished he could have seen a bit more of the world and then gone home. Because, after all, home was home. Everybody needed home at some point in their lives.

"M'sieur Schumacher!"

Qui, thought Johann Daniel, eyes still shut tight, to be called Monsieur again, the plain old French Mr rather than the title Peter had granted him – His Excellency the High Librarian of All the Russias.

"M'sieur Schumacher!"

Monsieur Schumacher, His Excellency the High Librarian of All the Russias, opened his eyes and let go of the shelf at the same time.

Being the cleverest man in all Russia he wondered as he fell if this would be the end, while still keeping a tight hold of the book. But instead of crashing on to the Great Library's stone floor he was grabbed by Alexei's mighty arms. Once fully grown, Alexei would have been able to catch him and remain standing but he was a still-growing giant so together they collapsed to the floor, Johann Daniel's cloak covering them as they lay in a spaghetti heap of arms and legs.

Silence returned to the library.

"M'sieur Schumacher? Alexei?"

"Watch he doesn't try and bite you, Alexei."

"Oh, shush, Nikolai."

The cloak moved and Johann Daniel's head appeared.

"Would you take this, please, while we untangle ourselves." He handed Kat the book.

"What is it?"

"A collection of travellers' tales from around the Empire – a useful read if you're planning a journey across Russia."

Kat stared at it. "How did you…"

"He's heavier than he looks." Alexei pushed Johann Daniel upright.

"Thank you, my boy," said Johann Daniel and shook his cloak.

Nikolai took a step back. "I don't bite, boy," said Johann Daniel. He turned to Kat.

"My dearest Katinka Dashkova…" – apart from Tzar Peter he was the only person to use her full name, which now made him the only one – "… how very timely of you and your friends to arrive like that."

He coughed. "Parched – time for tea. Come, children."

Seemingly none the worse for his fall, he marched off down the aisle heading for a small door, his cloak billowing behind him. "Of course I knew you were coming, just not when exactly."

Johann Daniel disappeared through the door into a dark room. Alexei ducked down to fit through after him. Nikolai hesitated. "He's spooky – I'm not going in there. What if it's a trap?"

"Don't worry," said Kat as she followed Alexei – there was no need for her to duck, "there was plenty of garlic in our dinner, that should keep him off."

"Really? Will it?"

But Kat had gone. Nikolai heard her giggle.

"Oh, damn you to hell, lumpen," he muttered. It was what they called anyone who wasn't a dwarf, lumpens, big, stupid humans who thought they were the 'normal' ones. Kat wasn't really a lumpen but what else could he call her? She wasn't like him was she? But she wasn't like Them. She was different too. One of the Tzar's Curiosities – Curiosity Kat. He smiled.

"Come on, Nikolai – it's tea time."

He liked hearing Kat say his new name. He liked her as well. Despite her teasing, and her temper, there was something about her. Perhaps he should stick with these two, the giant and the girl with the crooked back. After all, what else was he going to do? He just hoped the vampire wouldn't be coming to the Urals as well.

As he stepped through the door, Johann Daniel tugged back the curtain covering a large window at the end of the room. Morning light flooded in.

"Love the morning," said Johann Daniel to no-one in particular. "Every time I wake and see the sun I feel blessed to walk this earth. God save us from a dull day."

He turned around to speak directly to the three children, now standing in a row in the middle of the room.

"And he most certainly does that in this palace doesn't he – never a dull moment in the service of the Tzar."

"Tzarina," suggested Kat.

"Hmmm," said Johann Daniel, "yes, the Tzarina. Change in Russia always comes with days, maybe weeks, God forbid months of blood-letting. They're a blood thirsty lot the Romanovs and all who surround them."

"Like vampires," said Kat and nudged Nikolai.

"What? Yes, well, perhaps. So what are we going to do with you three then?"

"We want to go to the Urals."

"The Urals? That's a long journey, a dangerous one – the steppe is no place for children."

"How far?"

"What?"

"How far is it from St Petersburg to the Urals?"

Johann Daniel shook his head. "The best part of 2,000 versts, too far for children."

"How far?"

Johann Daniel sighed. "Yes, of course – I'd forgotten."

He shuffled over to a large chest of drawers, opened one and pulled out a rolled piece of parchment big enough to suit its home.

"The largest map ever made of Russia and its great empire," said Johann Daniel. He unrolled it on the table, rummaged in another draw and took out a long thin piece of wood.

"Now let's see," he said. "Where to in the Urals, my dear girl?"

"Yegoshikha, where the Yegoshikha and Kama Rivers meet, where my heart belongs."

Johann Daniel looked up at Kat. "You really mean it, don't you?" He didn't wait for an answer. "How do you know about Yegoshikha?" And this time he waited.

"I found out." Kat wouldn't look at him. Johann Daniel had become if not a father to her then certainly a very fond uncle. He was the kindest person she'd ever met, although she was sure her parents would be just as kind. She just couldn't remember very well. Which worried her because memory was one of her strong points. Maybe it was because her memory had improved as she'd grown up.

Kat didn't want to admit her crime to Johann Daniel. She had broken into the records office – Peter the Great was a stickler for everything being written down and recorded – and looked up where she came from, Yegoshikha, this village in the Ural Mountains, her father, Ivan Dashkov, her mother Irina, her dear Papa and Mama. There was an 'X' marked next to their names – she would like to ask Johann Daniel what that stood for but that would mean telling him what she'd done. Besides which she knew where her parents were and that was all that mattered.

She often tried to think about them, shutting her eyes and frowning in concentration, thin lines sketching across her forehead. Her father, she was sure, was tall and strong but with kind eyes. Her mother always smiling and humming a song as she went about her daily tasks. She couldn't precisely picture their faces. There was a faded image in her mind and she knew if she didn't get home soon it would get fainter and fainter until she couldn't see them at all.

"On occasions," said Johann Daniel, "you have to do things that break rules. Sometimes there are good reasons for doing that."

He turned his attention back to the map. It was Johann Daniel who taught her to read, Johann Daniel who told her stories about this great land, about its rivers and lakes and mountains and animals and its people, of which she was one.

"Unlike me," he would say, "you are a Russian Katinka Dashkova, you have Russia's blood flowing through every corner of you."

She didn't feel very much like a Russian. She felt that she was just Katinka, her own self. Chance or bad luck had made her one of the Tzar's Circus and they came from all over the world. But if she hadn't been a Curiosity, she wouldn't have learnt how to read or met Johann Daniel. The Tzar ordered she attend daily classes with his daughters. She went to their ballet lessons and while they giggled and clowned around, she danced and learnt. In reading classes she studied hard while the young Grand Duchesses giggled some more. And all the time she tried not to wonder if they were giggling at her.

She knew why she was allowed to receive an education many noble families could not afford for their children. She overheard the Tzar telling Johann Daniel one day; Peter the Great wanted Katinka Dashkova in class with his daughters to remind Natalya and Maria, the Grand Duchesses who would one day marry kings, how lucky they were. She was an example, a Curiosity and would never be allowed to be anything else in the Tzar's Court.

"So to be precise as you wish Katinka, by my calculations it is one thousand, eight hundred and seventy-one versts from St Petersburg to where the

Kama and Yegoshikha rivers meet. Still a very long way."

"We're going," said Kat and crossed her arms. Alexei copied her, Nikolai shrugged then nodded.

"I see," said Johann Daniel. "Well then, we've work to do and not much time to do it."

8

They spent their final hours in the Winter Palace in Johann Daniel's favourite room. It was his gift from the Tzar – Peter the Great being very, very good; marvel one day, monster the next.

The room opened off one end of the library. By the standards of the Palace it was no great size but once the curtains were drawn tight it transformed into the star attraction.

"There," said Johann Daniel. He was pointing at a star, a golden star because it was just that – gold. A map of the stars decorated the ceiling, a dome rising above the room, each star cut from gold leaf and positioned in the correct place in this miniature galaxy. They glittered in the flickering light of the candles.

"That's the North Star, Polaris – that shows you where north lies. You want to go east so look for…" his finger searched the painted sky… "…there, Orion – Orion rises in the east and sets in the west. By night you use the stars to guide you – learn them well, my children."

"But what if we travel by day?"

"Night is safer – at least from human danger. Wolves and bears hunt in the dark so beware. You must judge – you are bright children, you have survived in the Palace, and that's a strength to take into the world outside these walls. You will have my map, my gift to you – you must take it with you always, you must promise me that. It'll guide you… just as the sun and stars will."

"How?"

Johann Daniel ignored Kat's question.

"If you travel by day, ride in the direction the sun rises. Go east, keep going east until you see the Urals – when you reach the mountains turn south. There are two mountains to look out for, named for their shape. When you see Bear Mountain – you must look for it at sunrise – then you're getting close, take the valley that runs east, heading deeper into the Urals.

"After a few days, three, maybe four, you will see the Mountain of the Crown, turn south again and follow the Kama River and you will come, God willing, to Yegoshikha."

"And there I will find Mama and Papa," said Kat, her question forgotten.

"And live happily ever after," said Nikolai with a sneer on his face that suggested he didn't believe in happy endings. Not in the Tzar's Russia.

"Hmmm," said Johann Daniel.

They studied the stars, trying to paint them into their minds. Then they sat and listened as Johann Daniel offered a life-time's worth of collected advice about life on the road, the dangers, the do's and don'ts, the custom at inns, the custom in remote villages, how to address a Cossack chief without insulting him, the sound a wolf pack makes when it's hungry and ready to hunt, how to play dead if approached by an angry bear.

"Easy for you to say," muttered Nikolai.

Kat's head was spinning and Zhukov's arrival with bread and cheese was a relief. He whispered with Johann Daniel while they ate. The tall, stooped

Frenchman, he was all elbows and jagged edges, raised a long-fingered hand and rested it on one of Zhukov's broad shoulders.

"You are a good man, Sergeant, a good man indeed."

Zhukov had 'borrowed' one of the small Palace carriages into which the three children could squeeze. He left them to rest while he loaded it with any supplies he could get his hands on and furs from the store room.

Zhukov was waiting at nightfall when they crept down to the courtyard. He harnessed in place an old horse, one whose disappearance would not soon be noticed.

"Treat the old mare kindly – she will not go quick but she will go far if you look after her."

He sniffed the air. It was dark, and chilly. Summer was beginning to slide away. "You must not dally," said Zhukov. "If winter arrives before you have shelter it will kill you."

Zhukov helped Nikolai into the carriage. The mare snorted, its steamy breath rose into the blackness. Zhukov held out a hand and Kat used it to clamber in. Alexei needed no helping hand. He took the reins.

"Go, quick – I've the Guards turn their back for

five minutes. Get out of the city as soon as possible. You are the Tzar's property so they may send a troop after you – if anyone notices you're gone. There will be a reward on your heads when they do find out. Be careful."

"Here…" Johann Daniel, wrapped in his black cloak beneath a pale face and looking more vampirish than ever, pulled one hand out and offered a small bag of coins and a folded piece of paper sealed with a drop of candle wax. "Take this Katinka Dashkova – open it when you reach the Yegoshikha River."

"What is it?" Kat pushed it inside her shirt – she'd changed into britches and a man's shirt that covered her back. Her hair was gathered beneath a cap. She wore a cloak, one of Johann Daniel's old ones, wrapped tight around her. Beneath it she held her red ballet pumps, a gift from the Tzar himself after she danced for him.

Johann Daniel shook his head. "Not till the Yegoshikha River."

"Thank you," she said, "for everything."

Zhukov raised his hand and smacked the mare. "Now go – God speed – find a better place than this." He smacked again and the mare began to move.

"Hah," said Alexei and flicked the reins. The mare obeyed orders and picked up speed at once. To Kat her hooves clattered over the cobbles like an alarm call to every room in the Winter Palace. Surely someone would see them – raise the alarm, the gates would be shut, they would be imprisoned to face The Terror and his instruments of torture.

But no-one stirred. A guard beneath the arch leading from the courtyard turned away as they approached. If he was asked, he'd seen nobody pass.

They gathered speed as they clopped out of the Winter Palace, her home for eight years and, if she was being honest with herself, the only home Kat had ever really known.

9

It was Nikolai's suggestion they slow down through the still streets of St Petersburg. If they rushed, he said, it would turn heads, attract attention – what are they fleeing from? Take it slow as if we are going about normal business.

"Just three Curiosities running away from the Tzarina and heading off to certain death somewhere out on the steppe," he said.

"Well don't come then," snapped Kat.

"Pah," said Nikolai with a shrug. "I can't miss my own funeral can I?"

"I'll dig your grave for you."

"You don't have the strength – you're a girl."

"Why you snivelling little bag of dung..." Kat raised her fists.

"Stoi," barked Alexei. He pulled on the reins and the old mare stopped.

He turned to face them. "If you two are going to be like this then you can get out and walk – all the way to the Urals for all I care."

The mare snorted and shook her head as if agreeing with the young giant. They sat there for a minute, two. The street was deserted. The Guards patrolled the city at night – if they stayed for too long someone would get interested. But Alexei sat tight, reins gripped in huge hands.

"Well?" he said.

"Sorry, Alexei," said Kat.

"Don't say sorry to me."

"Oh come on – he started it, he's just a scared little boy."

"I'm sorry, Kat – I am sorry."

Nikolai's reply took them by surprise – even Nikolai himself it seemed. Another silence descended, one minute, two…

"And I'm sorry Nikolai – I shouldn't have said those things."

"Just because we live surrounded by cruel people, it doesn't mean we have to become like them," insisted Alexei. "That's what my late father always said."

"At least you knew your father," mumbled Kat.

"Yeah," agreed Nikolai. "Sometimes I look around the Palace dwarves and wonder which of them might be my father, and then I hope it's none of them."

He sniffed loudly.

"Are you crying, Nikolai?" Kat prodded him in the ribs. "You are aren't you?"

"No," said Nikolai, wiping his nose on his sleeve. "I never cry – crying's for girls."

"Why you…"

"Noooo," yelled Alexei. "Enough."

His voice bounced off the wall and rolled along the street.

Kat and Nikolai looked at him open mouthed. Kat was first to put hers back into action.

"Quick – get moving. Now we really will have the Guard after us, you big blundering bear." She tipped back her head and laughed, Nikolai joined in. Alexei flicked his wrists and the old mare hunched her shoulders and moved them on. Kat was sat close to Alexei and could feel his body shaking – she realised he too was laughing but trying to hide it. She prodded him in the ribs and a great guffaw escaped his mouth.

The laughing stopped when they left St Petersburg behind. The city ended abruptly. One minute they were in it, the next they weren't. The dark closed around them. Kat shuffled closer to Alexei and felt Nikolai press against her. They wrapped furs around themselves and carried on into the night.

Kat felt warm, and with Alexei and Nikolai either side, she felt safe. For those first few hours after leaving St Petersburg, dozing on and off as the old mare plodded through the night, Kat felt better than she had for a long time.

She woke with a start, her dream brought to a sudden end. She had been dancing, down one of the Palace's endless corridors, people were chasing her, shouting horrible things at her but she was dancing away from them, twirling and leaping out of their reach, getting closer and closer to a bright light at the end of the corridor.

The low sun shone into her eyes, rising into the eastern sky. Her neck felt stiff. Nikolai's head rested on her left shoulder. He was asleep. She nudged him and his head slid forward, jolting him awake. He snorted and Kat giggled.

"Uragghh," he said.

"Good morning to you," she replied. She turned to Alexei and placed a hand on his arm. "Sorry, you've had no sleep. Shall we stop, let you rest – where are we?"

"Whoooah," suggested Alexei to the old mare. His voice was soft, kind… well done, old girl, it said, time for a rest.

He unbuckled the reins and led her off the track into a grassy meadow that ran along one side. On the other a wood accompanied the track towards the horizon where they could make out the beginnings of a lake, a trace of water shimmering happily beneath the rising sun. Alexei hobbled the horse and left her to a breakfast of fresh grass.

Alongside the track they unrolled Johann Daniel's map, Nikolai placing a stone carefully on each corner. They stared at it in wonder, its web of finely drawn lines and small sketches of grey mountains, endless rivers, vast forests, carefully spelt out towns and villages and churches with onion domes all colours of the rainbow. It looked like a land of make-believe.

Plenty was left to the imagination. In between the landmarks, spidery roads stretched across unknown land, verst upon verst of wilderness and wildness.

"Where are we?" wondered Kat.

"Here, I think," said Alexei, stubbing a meaty finger on the map.

"Careful," said Nikolai. He didn't want to touch the map.

Kat shook her head. "No, that's not right – we've travelled all night we must be further on."

She traced her finger along the route Johann Daniel had suggested. They had turned off the Moscow road a few versts outside St Petersburg. The Moscow road was the simplest way to the east but it was not direct and more importantly was much busier – they were less likely to bump into any Guards or attract unwanted attention this way.

"There," said Alexei, pointing on down the track. "That water, that's Lake Lagoda. We're here."

He prodded the same point as before.

Kat looked at where they were, where they had to get to, what lay between them and Yegoshikha, and before she could stop it a sob burst out of her mouth.

She put her hands over her face, taken by surprise by the wave of anguish sweeping through her body; she could feel their hopelessness pressing down on her. Her head throbbed.

"What?"

She shook her head. "We'll never make it… we should go back, we must go back, what are we doing, look at us, three… three people from the Tzar's Circus… three hopeless Curiosities…"

She let out another sob then held her hand over her mouth. Alexei reached a long arm around her. "Kat, no…"

Nikolai butted in. He spoke quietly, staring at the map. "Without hope, there's nothing, just a big hole in your life. That's why you get up in the morning, because you have to hope today will be better, today will be the day. And if it isn't… you keep hold of your hope, tuck it in your pocket. Tomorrow will be better."

Kat sniffed. Alexei stood up.

"I'll get the horse."

"I'll do the map," said Nikolai.

Kat sniffed again.

"D'you know," said Nikolai as he rolled up the

map with more care and attention than he'd paid to anything in his life. There was something about it that demanded proper care and attention. "I've ridden in this carriage before."

Kat stood up and followed him back to the carriage. The wave had washed over her. It was gone. Alexei tied the mare back in place. The carriage rocked as he climbed in. He reached out a hand and helped first Kat then Nikolai up.

"Did you ever do the Christmas singing?" continued Nikolai. "There was this one time Tzar Peter himself stomped into our sleeping quarters, picked me from my bed, slung me over his shoulder and marched down to the courtyard where this carriage was.

"He wrapped a fur cloak around me, pushed a couple of musicians in alongside me and led us off round the streets of Petersburg. Waiting outside the Palace was a choir, one of the cathedral choirs, all shivering in their church robes. The Tzar led us, taking those giant strides of his – remember?"

Nikolai chuckled at the memory. "We stopped outside the houses of his favourite Duchesses and Princesses and he made us sing Christmas songs – I had to start off and then the rest would join in. If he wasn't happy, he chucked snowballs at us and made his Guards do the same.

"We would sing until the lady of the house appeared at the balcony and threw down a handful of coins as a Christmas thank you. Tzar Peter wouldn't let us pick them up – leave them, he roared, leave them for my people to find on Christmas morning and then they will love me even more.

"He kept us out all night, until the cock crowed. I was frozen, fingers were blue, I was shaking with cold. I remember it was this carriage because feel this…"

He took Kat's hand, lent forward and guided it along the front of the carriage. The wood was scratched like someone had tried to carve their name with a knife.

"A bear did that – two bears were made to pull the carriage, whipped till they walked on two feet. At the end, back in the courtyard, a footman came to take the reins off and one bear got free, started swinging these huge paws around and roaring – pure rage it was, thrashing at anything in sight.

"He took a swing at me but scratched the trap. I just sat there – think I was frozen with terror… that really happens you know.

"But there was something else keeping me there – I wanted to see what happened because I'd watched what they'd done to this bear. They whipped and baited and teased and tortured him, but he never gave up – I think he was saying to himself all night 'Remember you're a great Russian bear, remember you're a great Russian bear.' And when his chance came, he had his revenge."

Nikolai paused. "Oh my, oh my, oh my, it was bloody – another swing… boof…" Nikolai swung his hand… "took the footman's head clean off. It bounced across the cobbles. Then the bear got on all fours, as God intended, and ran, straight out the courtyard. They hunted him but never found a trace – some say he fell in the Neva and was swept away, others he was a spirit and dissolved into the night, others say he got away, clean away, back to the woods where he still lives, hunting humans, still taking his revenge."

"Is that meant to scare me?" said Kat.

"No… it's meant to…"

"I know Nikolai, thank you – I feel better. I won't give up, no matter how they treat us – I promise you."

She turned to Alexei. "And I promise you, Alexei."

She put her hands out and they each took one,

Nikolai's was small, even smaller than hers, Alexei's was as big as a bear paw.

"Sometimes growing up scares me," she said. "I've been scared for a long time – that feeling in my tummy... D'you get that? I want to make it go away... forever."

Alexei grunted and snapped the reins.

10

Have you ever heard a wolf howl?

Kat might have before she came to the Winter Palace, but she was too young to remember. Nikolai and Alexei certainly hadn't. They'd seen a wolf. They'd seen all sorts of animals in the Palace – Tzar Peter collected them as much as he did humans. The Palace wolf never howled, instead it silently paced the corridors as if searching for something. Nikolai wanted to set it free, open a door and point it into the street, but he was too afraid of what might happen if he was caught in the act.

It had been a long day, watching the mare plod onwards down the track. For a long time Lake Lagoda glistened on their left. It was warm and they stopped for an hour to let the mare drink while they splashed in the shallows. It felt like a holiday.

That mood ebbed away as they left the lake behind and the track took them deeper and deeper into the forest. They saw no-one, not a sign of life, passed no cottages, saw no smoke from home fires, just the track, going on and on.

They heard the howl as dusk was beginning to ease the day away. It's a sound like no other. It gets inside you, rolls around your head and drains blood from your face. "You are wolf white," they say in Russia when someone's had a scare.

"I'm afraid," said Alexei, his knuckles white as they gripped the reins.

The howl came again, echoing through the trees and invading the carriage, creeping around the children and chilling them to the bone.

"You?" said Nikolai. "Afraid?"

The horse whinnied and shook her head, as if suggesting travelling through the forest after dark was a bad idea.

"What's there to be afraid of for a big lump like you? Any wolf comes near you and you can bash it on the head with one of those boulders you call fists."

"If they come there won't be one, they'll come together. A pack – the wolf never travels alone and never attacks alone."

"Well, that wasn't a hunting call and you're not alone either," said Kat.

"Yeah," said Nikolai, "one look at us should scare them away."

He snorted in satisfaction at his words and turned the collar of his coat up in an attempt to disguise the shiver that followed. It was a shiver of fear. He was scared too but there was no way on God's earth he would admit it.

Another howl hurried towards them, this time from the other side of the track. Kat scanned the gloomy trees. There was no sign of anything. She didn't feel scared – well, no more than usual. Real things didn't scare her, not after all she'd experienced. No, it was fear of the unknown that had tried to seize her when they gathered around the map earlier... all that way to go with who knows what waiting at the end. If they ever made it to the end.

"They rip you to shreds you know," said Alexei,

his eyes fixed on the track ahead. "One of the Tzar's hunters told me. He'd been in the forests; the great eastern forests some say have no end – they say no man has ever come to their end…"

"Someone told me they end at the very edge of the earth itself," interrupted Nikolai.

Kat shook her head but said nothing. This wasn't the time to try and educate Nikolai – right now Kat had to get Alexei through the night.

They'd decided to take Johann Daniel's advice and travel at night for the first few days as there was less chance of meeting anyone who might get curious and start asking awkward questions.

"This hunter," said Alexei, determined to finish his story, "had a brother with him. They lost their horses so were on foot and this wolf pack started hunting them. They got separated, the hunter and his brother – and you know what the wolves did?"

Nikolai shook his head. His mouth was open, every bit of him gripped by Alexei's tale.

"They decided the brother was the weaker one, so they left the hunter and chased the brother, all of them. They're clever, wolves – they go for the weak because it's more dangerous to try and attack the strong. You see? The hunter said he heard his brother's screams as…"

"Enough," barked Kat.

"Ohhh," said Nikolai, "no, go on Alexei – what happened?"

"You know what happened," said Kat. "It's not a fairy story and neither is this. Stop."

"What?" said Alexei, still not moving his gaze from its rigid stare up the track.

"Stop – I need to get something, something that'll keep the wolves away."

"What?" wondered Nikolai.

"Wait and see."

"No," said Alexei. "We must keep going."

"Right," said Kat and stood up.

"Kat – what you doing?"

She didn't answer. Instead she stepped over Nikolai and leapt out of the carriage.

She landed on her right foot, bending at the knee to absorb the shock of the landing. The old mare travelled at a slow pace which made it an easy escape for Kat. She put her arms out to make sure of her balance and then spun round, as if mid-dance, to face the carriage and the boys.

"Kat, get back in – quick." Alexei stopped the carriage and tore his gaze from the track. He shot nervous glances into the woods.

Kat ignored him.

"Nikolai, I need to you to gather a bundle of wood."

"What me? Go into the trees? No thank you very much – I'm not going to be a wolf's dinner. If you want it, you get it."

"Kaaaat – get in," begged Alexei.

"Huh," snorted Kat. "Some menfolk you two are."

And with that she spun round and leapt over the narrow trench dividing the track from the wood. She peered through the trees – truth be told she was a little frightened.

There was reason to be afraid. Russians fear wolves because they are nature's finest hunters, and between the three of them they had no more than Alexei's strength and the hunting knife Zhukov had tucked into their roll of furs.

But they also had Johann Daniel's brains and Kat's courage/pig-headedness (sometimes it's hard to tell the two apart).

"I'll keep watch for you, Kat," said Nikolai, standing up in the trap and clutching the knife.

"Huh," snorted Kat again and got on with collecting the wood. As she bent to scoop up each stick she felt the hairs on the back of her neck stand up. Every time she straightened up she expected to see the yellow eyes of a hungry wolf fixed on her.

She could hear noises deeper in the wood, the sounds of a forest as night approaches, rustling leaves, occasional squawks but no more howling. Which meant the wolf pack had either moved on. Or decided it was time to hunt. Wolves make no sound when they have work to do.

Kat was breathing quickly and it was not through tiredness. She gathered her bundle of sticks and leapt back across the trench. Even that small divide made her feel a little safer.

"What you doing?" Nikolai's attention switched from the woods to Kat – he was one of life's watchers, nothing escaped his sharp eye.

Kat ignored him and rummaged in the pack Johann Daniel had loaded into the trap. She took out a small leather pouch and a flint, dug around a little more and tugged out a couple of rags. From beneath the pack she took a bundle of thin rope.

"Knife," she said and held up a hand to Nikolai. He handed it over and she cut two lengths of rope. She sorted the wood into two bundles, secured each with rope and then wound the rags around the top. From the pack she took a small bottle and dribbled a little blue liquid on each rag, then did the same with yellow powder from a second bottle. She replaced each bottle carefully, making sure the stoppers were shut tight.

She crouched down behind the trap.

"What ARE you doing?" asked Nikolai again as she disappeared from his sight.

Kat laid the bigger bundle next to a rock on the edge of the road and began to strike the flint hard against the rock.

Curiosity forced Nikolai out of the trap – nothing would make Alexei move.

"Ohhh," said Nikolai as a spark from the flint darted onto the bundle.

"Whoooofff," went the bundle and Kat picked it up and held the flame above her head.

"Sorcery," said Nikolai.

"No, science," said Kat.

"Eh?" wondered Nikolai.

Kat tied the bundle to the back of the carriage. "There," she said. "That'll burn for a few hours and then the other will see us through the night – no wolf will touch us now."

"Fire – wolves are terrified of fire," said Nikolai. "But how…"

Kat clambered back into the carriage and reached a hand down for Nikolai.

"Come," she said.

"The old vampire – he's no vampire, he's a wizard isn't he?"

"Hah," said Alexei and flicked the reins. The old mare whinnied but did as Alexei asked.

"Come on, Nikolai," said Kat.

"Is he? Is he a wizard?" He made no effort to get back in the carriage. "Tell me."

Kat sighed. "Yes, he's a wizard." She'd say anything to get in him back in.

"I knew it," shouted Nikolai and ran after the carriage. He jumped easily on to the back – his legs might be shorter than most but they were strong.

Among the other dwarves he was known as the Flea because of the height he could jump. A flea can leap 200 times its own height – Nikolai couldn't manage that but did once win a round of applause from the Tzar for jumping onto a horse from a standing start. The horse had been led into the middle of the banquet room after the 27th course – grilled sparrows with snail stuffing – and left there. Nobody knew quite why.

He scrambled over the bags and slid into his seat. "I knew it – I knew he wasn't normal..."

"Who is?" grunted Alexei, eyes back on the track. It wasn't meant as a question so Nikolai didn't answer it. Besides Nikolai wasn't listening to anything except his own imagination.

"A wizard – wow oh wow... what other spells did he tell you? Are they in that bag? Can you make me invisible? Imagine what it would be like being invisible – I'd go back to the Palace and haunt them, haunt them like a ghost – in the middle of night I'd whip off their bedcovers and scream... I'd slam doors in people's faces then trip them up when they came through, I'd... I'd find the snootiest countess and tickle them, find the nastiest count and shake his arm when he's holding a glass of kvass next to the Tzar, tip it all over the Tzar – he'd have their hands cut off…"

"That's not very nice."

"No, well, I mean… I wouldn't do that – I'd help people as well, I would."

Nikolai paused to draw breath and caught the look Kat was giving him. Even Alexei had switched his attention to Nikolai.

"Well I would… promise."

He felt embarrassed so turned his head and spat over the side of the carriage.

"So I'm not perfect – cut off my head and call me headless."

Kat shook her head.

"Oh, it's just a bit of spit – you should try it sometime, might let off a bit of that steam boiling away inside you… you're like a kettle you are, Kat the Kettle, bubble, bubble, KABOOM."

Nikolai threw his hands in the air, then turned his head and spat again, this time furiously.

Kat felt bubbling inside her, rising through her throat, steaming along her arms, clenching her fists. She drew back her right fist. He was so annoying, not like Alexei. She never wanted to hit Alexei. He never made her boil over. She really wanted to hit Nikolai.

But she didn't.

If they'd still been in the Palace she was sure she would have. Out here though, in the middle of nowhere, verst after verst from anywhere, it felt different. This wasn't Palace life anymore. They'd left the Jolly Company and its horrors behind. She unclenched her fist feeling like she'd won.

Nikolai nudged her with his elbow. "Kettle Kat! Good one, eh?"

He grinned at her.

"Do you really believe in wizards?"

He nodded. "And if we've a wizard watching over us we're sure to get all the way to the Urals. That was amazing with the fire – are you his apprentice?"

"Apprentice?"

"Yes, learning to be a witch."

"Me?"

"Yes."

"No."

"I don't believe you."

"Look Nikolai… I can't do magic, I'm only me… I…" began Kat, "… oh, never mind."

A howl drifted towards them, but this time from far away. The wolves had moved on.

11

They didn't hear another wolf for the remainder of the night. Although that may have been down to Alexei's snoring drowning out any sound within earshot. A small earthquake, one of those tremors that rattle tea cups and wobble wigs, wouldn't have matched Alexei's snoring.

"Shall I elbow him?" wondered Nikolai.

"No," said Kat, "leave him be – he's exhausted. Let me take the reins, you sleep."

Nikolai shook his head. "I can go all night – used to it. We had to be ready for the Tzar's call any minute, day or night. His guards slept, his dwarves didn't – always ready to serve the Tzar by being laughed at. Once went three nights with no sleep when..."

He shrugged. "That was my life then – not any more, left that behind. You sleep."

Kat shook her head. "I won't leave you on your own."

"I'm all right on my own."

"I know but, well, you don't have to be."

"All right then – but only if you tell me a story. I love stories... tell me one of his, the Wizard's, he must have told you some proper good ones."

Kat looked down at him. She could never tell from his voice whether he was being serious, or if he was teasing her. His face was easier to read. He looked like a boy ready for his bedtime story. So she began.

And when she finished the first one, he asked for another and another, and he questioned her about them. Why couldn't the lion get the thorn out of its own paw? Did the wolf survive? Did the children grow up to live happily ever after?

"Johann Daniel never told me... I like to think they did – that's what he said, 'What do you think, Katinka?' I think they did because if you can't imagine a happy ending how will you ever find one?"

"Tell me another – one about wolves..."

"I can't Nikolai, I'm tired."

"Pah, you'd never have made it as one of the Tzar's dwarves – neither of you, beauty or the snoring beast."

"Beauty?"

Nikolai turned away, looking into the dark woods.

"Well, you are, aren't you, when you dance – most beautiful thing I saw in that Palace."

He was mumbling so Kat wasn't sure she heard him right. She thought about asking him to repeat himself. Nikolai spat over the side.

"Yeah, well," he said, "you get some sleep."

She rested her head against Alexei and smiled to herself as she fell asleep.

When she woke she could see the sky. It was bright blue. She blinked. They weren't moving. The twitter of bird song floated above her. The carriage was in a clearing in the forest – they were off the track. The old mare, its head bowed, was chomping on the dark green grass that lay thick across the clearing. There was no sign of Alexei or Nikolai. Kat felt a flicker of alarm.

"We're under here." Nikolai's voice came from

beneath the carriage. She climbed down. The boys had spread the furs on the ground. Alexei was already asleep.

"We'll stay here a few hours," said Nikolai. "It's what me and Alexei thought, have a good rest, all of us – and the old girl. Go on when the sun reaches there."

He pointed straight up into the sky.

"I'm hungry," said Kat.

"Not as much as he is," said Nikolai, gesturing a thumb at Alexei. "Should have heard his tummy rumbling, thought the world was coming to an end."

Right on cue a long, low growl filled the space beneath the carriage.

"Sounds like it's getting angry now."

"We'll give him the rest of the bread when he wakes," decided Kat. "You and me can wait till we get to an inn or something."

She yawned and stretched out next to Alexei. "It's nice to lie down – I feel so tired."

"You sleep – I'll keep watch."

"Thank you, Nikolai," said Kat. Within a minute she was asleep.

* * *

Legs. One, two, three, four, five, six, seven, eight, nine. No, that can't be right. There couldn't be nine legs. Kat counted again. She'd reached five when she caught herself. She rubbed her eyes. Was she dreaming?

No, there were legs down one side of the carriage. She turned her head. And down the other side too. They were surrounded.

"Come out before we haul your butts out."

The voice was rough.

Kat shook Alexei.

"Huh?" he said.

"Alexei…" hissed Kat, "wake up."

Nikolai was awake – his eyes wide – but he lay still.

"What shall we do?" asked Kat. Nikolai said nothing, just stared at her, eyes now so big they seemed to take over his entire face.

Alexei sat up, forgot where they were and thudded his head into the bottom of the carriage.

"Urrggh," he said before adding, "owwww!" A stick was shoved beneath the carriage and rammed into his ribs.

"Last chance," came the voice. "Next time it'll be a scythe and we'll cut you up for our dinner."

"Cannibals?" wondered Kat, her eyes widening to match Nikolai's.

"No, serfs... peasants," said Alexei, rubbing his side. "We better do as they say."

He rolled onto all fours and crawled out.

"Holy mother of God – what is that?" A different voice, a higher pitch but rough as well.

"Stand back – I'll deal with this." The first voice again.

Kat nudged Nikolai. "Come on."

Nikolai did as he was told and crawled after Alexei.

There was a hoot of laughter.

"What the..."

"A freak show..."

"Kill them..."

"Yeah, quick Sergei, use the axe... get the big one first..."

"Wait... NO..." the first voice again, commanding... "wait. They'll belong to someone, one of the masters, we'll be rewarded for returning them. Take them – we'll hear their story in the village... get some rope around them... tie them together."

Kat saw hands reach down and pull Nikolai to his feet. Someone smacked a hand against the back of his head.

They were more cautious with Alexei. One of the peasants had a pitchfork which he used to prod Alexei. The giant boy growled but staggered to his feet and stood swaying as rope was bound around him. He was weak with lack of food – an Alexei with a full belly would not let himself be taken without a fight.

Kat lay stock still. The serfs didn't seem to realise there was a third person beneath the carriage.

"Sergei…" the command voice again… "hitch that old mare up and bring the carriage in."

"Wait for me." Sergei's voice sounded anxious. "Wait… don't leave me alone…"

Kat watched. The legs were moving off, apart from two.

"Wait… there might be more of them… more giants… wait…"

"Sergei the Scared…" shouted one of the disappearing serfs. The rest of the legs disappeared from sight accompanied by a roar of laughter.

The left-behind legs, clothed in baggy trousers that

could have been cut from a sack, rose from a pair of dirty bare feet. The feet were pointing in the direction the others had gone so Kat ducked out the far side of the carriage and rummaged beneath the driver's seat. She found what she was looking for and tucked the knife into the waist band of her trousers.

Feeling a little better now she was armed – they would not catch her without a fight – she resumed her hiding place beneath the carriage. Kat watched the feet and took a deep breath, and another. If she slowed her breathing, Johann Daniel once told her, her mind would clear.

The feet turned and faced the carriage.

"Pffff," exhaled Sergei the Scared. The old mare whinnied, as if to remind Sergei what he was supposed to be doing. Kat saw the feet take a little jump at the noise – he really was scared. He scampered across the clearing towards the horse, which in turn edged further away. The old mare was not going to make it easy for Sergei, which gave Kat time and space to put her plan into action.

On every carriage used by the Tzar, or his family, a couple of wooden planks are fitted underneath, next to the front wheels. It was a place to hide valuables or anything else you wanted to keep out of sight while on the road – it wasn't much but in a dangerous land it might buy a little time before the Guards came to the rescue.

Except here there were to be no Guards riding to the rescue, and even if there were, they wouldn't be rescuing Kat, Alexei and Nikolai.

Kat slipped her feet onto one of the planks and then pulled the top half of her body up onto the other. She was twisted at an awkward angle, her back making it impossible to squeeze all her top half onto the support of the plank. Her bottom dangled in space. It was uncomfortable and difficult to hold on. Whether she would be able to once the carriage began moving, shaking and grinding its way along the rough track… well, she wasn't at all sure.

But she had to try. She had to get to this village, rescue the boys. These serfs would either kill them or hand them over to the local noblemen who would in turn hand them to the Guards and that might prove a fate worse than death. That's what they said in Court about anyone sent to see The Terror.

Sergei coaxed the mare into place. The carriage creaked as he climbed in.

"C-c-c-come q-q-q-uick," he said, the fear of being alone punctuating his words as he urged the old mare to get going. So desperate was Sergei the Scared to get after his fellow villagers he never noticed the pile of furs beneath the carriage. They may still be there, in a remote clearing deep in the forest in a distant part of Russia.

Despite Sergei's best efforts, there was no great urgency in the mare's tread – and for that Kat was truly grateful.

If it had been a young, keen horse in harness, brisk and business-like, Kat would never have held on. Each turn of the wheels, each rut or rock the carriage lumbered over, jolted her body. The muscles in her arms screamed in protest. She could feel the plank rubbing against her back. It felt like it was burning. She gasped as the skin broke and felt a warm trickle of blood run down her back. She hung on.

She closed her eyes and searched her head for a day dream – the Urals, a hut in a clearing by a silver stream, Alexei repairing the roof, Nikolai fishing, her sitting on the doorstep singing as she brushed her hair. She felt the warm grass beneath her bare feet, the warm sun on her face, the warm blood running down her back, soaking into her shirt.

The knife, still secure in her waistband, dug into her flesh. She opened her eyes. Better to face it. She spoke to herself. "Hang on, Katinka, hang on."

12

The heavens opened. Kat watched Sergei the Scared's legs dart across the village square and disappear into a ramshackle hut.

With a groan she let go and flopped into the puddle beneath the carriage. The muddy water felt cool on her face. Her back stung, the rest of her body ached from top to toe.

She could see the rain beating against the ground, great drops drumming in the dust and turning it to mud. It made a noise like one of the Tzar's finest battalions marching across the Winter Palace parade ground.

Kat pushed herself onto all fours and crawled from beneath the carriage. She squatted beside it and glanced around the village. There wasn't much to it, and what there was wasn't up to much.

Huts ran around three sides of the square. They were low, made of trees felled from the forest, each with a front door and one small window. A slither of smoke rose from each. On the fourth side a larger building, a barn, stood next to the track that led back into the forest.

The double doors to the barn were shut with a block of wood secured across the front to keep them that way.

Kat stood up. Her head spun, she held the carriage to steady herself.

"Are you all right?"

Kat jumped as high as Sergei the Scared. She spun round to face the voice, one hand darting behind her to touch the reassuring handle of the knife.

"Oh, sorry – didn't mean to startle you."

A small girl was looking up at Kat. Her sodden hair hung over her shoulders, rain ran down her face leaving track marks as it cleaned off a layer of dirt. She wore a smock that was so covered in patches there might not be any of the original left. Her feet were bare.

She sniffed, then wiped her nose just to be sure.

"Are you with the big one and the little one?"

"Where are they?"

The girl pointed at the barn. Kat studied her.

"How old are you?"

"12 and a bit," said the girl.

"12... but you..."

"Are small, yes. There's little to eat here, most children in the village are skinny. The grown-ups take most of the food, say they need it to be strong to grow the crops and look after the animals so we can all have food. Except there never seems to be food for us. We wait and get thinner and don't grow."

For a moment her face hardened. There was anger there, thought Kat. Like the anger I have in me.

"Will you help me... help me get them out, the big one and the little one?"

The girl shrugged. Kat glanced around. This was taking too long, someone would soon come to inspect the carriage, see what bounty they'd recovered.

"They won't come out."

"What?"

"Not in this rain, and it'll bring night early –

grown-ups don't go out after dark. Too scared. They sent me to take the carriage into the barn."

Kat ducked back beneath the carriage and gestured for the girl to join her.

"What's that?"

She pointed at Kat's back. Kat felt a flush of anger.

"Blood, you're bleeding, you need to stop that."

"No time," snapped Kat.

The girl looked at the ground, her feet were nearly covered by the rising puddle.

"I'll help you."

"What?"

"Help you get the big one and the little one out, show you the way through the forest... I know the way."

"Why?"

"Because I want to come with you... me and Arkady."

"Arkady? Who's Arkady?"

"My little brother. I'm Olga. I'll help you get away and you take us with you."

"Why?"

"Do you have a mother?"

"What?" The rain beat heavier, drowning Olga's words.

"A MOTHER – DO YOU HAVE A MOTHER?"

Kat nodded. She lent in close to Olga. "That's where we're going, to find my mother – and my father."

"My mother's dead. My father ran away, left us with his brother – he treats his animals better than us. He tried to sell us once, to the Countess but the Countess didn't want us."

She shrugged. "There's nothing for us here. I would like to find a new mother."

"You only have one mother," said Kat.

Olga shrugged again.

"Will you take us?"

This time Kat shrugged. "All right."

She waited while Olga darted across the square. The rain was like a curtain, so heavy Olga became a blur within a few steps and was gone in a few more. Kat could only just see the outline of the barn.

She put her head down and ran for it, feeling the rain soak her in seconds. The roof overhung the barn door, offering a thin patch of shelter.

Kat pushed at the block of wood that kept the doors shut. It wouldn't budge.

A dark shape loomed out of the rain. The old mare snorted at Kat's failure to get the doors open and allow her under cover.

"I'll show you," said Olga. A boy, smaller than Olga, smaller than Nikolai, clung on to her hand.

"He's just a baby."

Olga ignored Kat. She leaned her right shoulder underneath the bar and with her left hand pulled hard at it. The bar swung up and she slid it to the ground.

"You just need to know how," said Olga. She pushed open one of the doors. It was dark inside. Kat cocked her head and listened. Singing, the sound of a soft voice singing a song she recognised.

"Nikolai!"

"Kat? Katinka?"

"Hold the mare – wait here, I'll get them out."

Olga, followed by Arkady, stepped back into the rain and stood either side of the old mare. Olga raised a hand and stroked her muzzle. Kat stepped into the darkness of the barn.

"Anyone else in here?"

"No, just me and Alexei… over here, in the corner. They beat us, hit us with sticks. You'll need the knife. We're tied up tight."

Kat nicked Nikolai's wrist with the knife as she cut the ropes. He sucked at it in between moaning at Kat, until he noticed her blood-soaked shirt. Her head was spinning.

"Kat… you're hurt."

"It's nothing – come on, let's get out of…"

* * *

Kat could hear the rain but she couldn't feel it. Her cheek rested against something soft. It smelt nice. She was lying on her front, her head hurt and the top of her back was throbbing.

"Stay still – you must stay still. You fainted."

Kat peered up at Olga who was crouching beside her.

"I've made a poultice for your wound – it will heal in a day."

"A what? We don't have a day."

Kat pushed herself up on her arms, tried to get on all fours.

"Lie down," said Olga. "I found the herbs and roots I need to mend you. I've mashed them up and covered your wound – rest and it will heal."

"A witch treats a witch – you've struck lucky, Kat!"

Nikolai sounded cheery. Kat turned her head in his direction. He was crouched over a fire, holding a couple of sticks with something jammed on the end of them.

"Mushrooms, she found us forest mushrooms so I'm cooking up a feast fit for a Tzar… well, fit for the Tzar's runaways."

"You know the Tzar?"

"We do, wee Arkady, very best of friends we are. At least we were – until he died."

"The Tzar is dead?"

"As a doorknob."

"Where's Alexei?"

"Sleeping," said Nikolai, "don't worry Kat – it's going to be all right. He needs food – we have food, the wee ones here pinched a couple of black loaves from their village and we have all the mushrooms we can eat. We'll rest here today, go on tonight, Olga says she can show us the way."

"Where are we?"

"In the forest, deep in the forest – Olga's secret cave. She says no-one will find us here. She found this cave and only she, Arkady and her best friend know about it. We're safe and by tomorrow morning we'll be well away from the village. Now rest – I'll wake you when the banquet's ready."

Nikolai turned back to the fire and hummed as he watched the mushrooms cook. He began to sing, softly, a lullaby every Russian child remembers their parents singing. Kat shut her eyes. She wanted to sleep, but it was bothering her that she couldn't recall her mother ever singing to her.

13

The forest was alive. A bird seemed to be singing from every tree, chirping its greeting to the sun peeking through every tiny break in the green canopy which shielded the forest floor. Sunny spotlights selected momentary stars, a fluttering butterfly, a zig-zagging bee and once even a darting weasel.

Kat and Olga walked ahead of the carriage, which was making even slower progress than usual. The track had not been used in a long while. Grass grew as high as the carriage wheels, tickling the girls' legs as they walked.

They were supposed to be watching for any holes or rocks that might injure the old mare or damage the carriage. Instead they let their feet do the looking – if they tripped or fell then they'd done their job – while

Olga pointed this way and that explaining a handful of the forest's thousands of secrets.

She told Kat where to look for roots that cure sore tummies, which plant has leaves to sooth a wound or a headache. Which berries…

"I know about the berries," interrupted Kat suddenly. A memory of a forest, a little girl – her – walking with someone else, her father, no, someone else, eyes, blue eyes… she shook her head. "Sorry, tell me more."

Olga explained how to spot the signs a bear was near – don't forget, she said, bears can climb trees so that is no way to escape them.

The forest was Olga's true home. She spent every minute she could in its shelter, anything to get away from the village. The women of the village passed down what they learnt from their mothers and grandmothers. Olga's mother had loved the forest and told her all she knew before she died. Her last words to Olga, whispered in her ear, were "never forget you can be free in the forest."

After three days of travelling the forest stopped. There was no slow thinning out, no trickle of trees to hint they were about to step out of its cover. It just ended. The trees stopped and the steppe began.

This did not bother the track which stretched on before them, on and on until it disappeared from sight. The old mare stepped out of the forest and the children followed – they were all walking except Nikolai, who was steering the carriage. He pulled on the reins.

"Whoa," he said.

Arkady reached up, patted the mare's nose and it nuzzled his ear in response.

"Where are we going, Olga?"

The others stepped from the forest and stared at the foreverness that lay ahead of them. Olga remained beneath the forest's comfort-blanket.

"Not there," she said.

"Olga?"

Kat took her hand.

"I – we, me and Arkady – we'll stay here… you go, you know which way is east better than I do."

"But Olga…"

"I can't… the forest is me… out there…" she waved a hand at the steppe… "that's not for me… it's too… too big."

She shook her head. "I don't know anyone who's been beyond the forest. You should stay with what you know." She nodded her head. "Yes, stay with what you know, that's sensible."

"But Olga if you stay nothing changes… you and Arkady you'll still be…"

"No," said Olga. "I'm not going back, not to the village. I can live here, me and Arkady, we can make a new life, like you're going to do…"

"Just you? But… but you're ch…"

"Children, yes, so?"

Kat nodded. She opened her arms and wrapped them around Olga. "Mark a tree… if we're ever passing we'll find you. One day… one day I'll hug you again."

"I won't forget you Katinka… you set us free."

"Pah," said Kat. She let Olga go and hugged Arkady.

"Get off…" he said. Kat pinched his cheek, like an old auntie to a much-loved nephew, and followed the boys out of the forest and on to the steppe.

When she turned back Olga and Arkady were still waving, standing just inside the treeline and waving. They got smaller and smaller until the last time Kat turned around, they were gone. She ran after the carriage. Nikolai lent back and offered his hand, Kat took it and scrambled aboard. She settled back into her usual place between the boys, and the old mare plodded on.

* * *

Does the steppe go on forever? There were some days when it felt like it.

The horizon never changed, long grass shifting in the breeze. Sometimes the track went down into a dip but always rose up the other side. Sometimes it went round a small grass-covered hill but always corrected itself and straightened again on the other side.

The first night – there now seemed no reason not to travel by day – none of them slept much. Curled up beneath the carriage, Kat felt like she was opening her eyes every five minutes and checking for legs surrounding them. In the morning Nikolai claimed to have heard wolves and not slept a wink.

Kat wasn't sure whether she believed him. Not that she thought he was lying, rather he was hearing things that weren't there. Nevertheless, that second evening, as the sun sunk low enough to set the steppe on fire, Kat prepared the flaming torches. She only put a sprinkle of liquid and powder on each, worried about running out before they reached the Urals.

She was even more worried about their food supply. They sat on the carriage and watched the sun disappear, chewing on small hunks of dry bread. They had enough bread for two, maybe three days. Enough water, carried in large flasks made of animal hide and hung from the side of the carriage, to last a few days beyond that. They must reach somewhere soon or they would be in serious trouble.

Johann Daniel had given Kat a couple more tricks to store up her sleeve, and one might come in use before too long (the other hopefully wouldn't ever for it was only for the direst emergency). Extra Trick One was another powder, but this was nothing magic just a mix of spices and dried herbs in a blue bottle (the Emergency Trick came in a green bottle).

"If you are ever starving, really starving," explained Johann Daniel of Extra Trick One, "take what water you can spare, pick handfuls of grass, boil it in the water – so you'll need to save some fire-starter – make a porridge and add the spices and herbs. The spices give it taste, the herb mix makes sure you can digest it and won't be sick.

"It'll keep you alive but your stomach won't take more than a few helpings – we're not animals, we are not made to live on grass…"

Kat looked around. Grass as far as she could see, in every direction. Nothing but grass. It was a relief when nightfall came and hid it from her.

14

"Kat... Kat..."

Nikolai shook Kat's shoulder. Then turned his attention to Alexei.

"Alexei... wake-up... wake-up..."

"Oh for all the trees in the forest," growled Alexei, "what is it, Nik?"

Alexei had started to call him by the shortened version of his name because it saved a few letters and, like his words, the letters they were made up of had to be used with care.

"I heard them, out there..." He pointed into the darkness, beyond the flickering light of the torches.

"The serfs?" wondered Kat, her head full of sleep.

Somewhere in the darkness the old mare whinnied. At night they hobbled her so she could graze nearby but wouldn't drift away.

"Nooo, wolves… the wolves are here… out there, listen…"

Alexei put his head to one side and closed his eyes.

"I'm certain of it… they're here, they're…"

"Shhh," said Alexei, "let me listen."

The mare whinnied again, this time with a definite note of alarm.

"Where is she?" said Kat, peering out from beneath the carriage.

"We should get the torches," said Nikolai.

The thought of stepping from beneath the carriage appealed to none of them. Being in the open, not knowing what was out there in the vastness of the steppe, hidden beyond the frail light of the torches, that was scary.

Kat ducked out and stood up. The night breeze stirred the grass, rustling it as if a deadly pack of wolves was creeping towards them.

Kat swallowed and reached behind her for the nearest torch – she daren't turn her gaze from the darkness. The breeze dropped. Not a single sound came from the steppe. Was it holding its breath, waiting for what it knew was going to happen? The Steppe had seen it all in the thousands and thousands of years it had been here, long, long before Russia claimed it within man-made borders.

Alexei joined Kat and reached across for the other torch. Nikolai stood between them, squinting to make out any shape in the darkness.

"Here you have it," said Alexei, handing the torch down to Nikolai.

"What about you?"

"I have my fists," said Alexei. Nikolai nodded, all the time keeping his eyes fixed ahead. All three of them were looking the same way, in the direction of the old mare's last whinny.

"Caaawwwwwwww."

Kat and Nikolai's torches jerked in alarm at the bird's startled cry, followed by furious flapping as it scrambled up into the night sky.

"A bird," said Kat and giggled in relief. Nikolai grinned at her. Alexei took a step forward, raising his fists and bunching them, ready to fight.

"Yes, but what woke it… what put it to flight?"

Kat swallowed and stepped forward alongside Alexei – more because she felt safer in his shadow than any real desire to find out why the bird had fled in such alarm.

She pushed the torch ahead of her. Her mouth was dry. She wanted to be curled up, back in the Kunstkamera's attic sleeping quarters in the Winter Palace. Better the devils you know than whatever devil was out here in the darkness of the steppe.

"Alexei…" she began.

"Shhhh," he hissed. He clicked his tongue a couple of times, the reassuring sound he made to the mare when he wanted to comfort her. Silence returned, a silence that roared in their ears.

Nikolai gripped his torch in both hands but it wasn't enough to stop it shaking. Kat cursed herself for forgetting the hunting knife. It was back in the carriage – was there time to race back and get it? The steppe let out its breath and the wind whispered through the grass.

The steppe knew the time had come.

The first growl was so low, little more than a gentle rumble from the back of the wolf's throat, that none of them were sure what they'd heard. Their ears knew but their brains refused to acknowledge it.

"Rrrrrrrrrrrrrr."

It died away.

"Ahhhhhhhh," sighed the steppe.

Alexei took a step forward, instinctively Kat did the same.

"Alexei?" she said.

"There," he said and leapt into the darkness.

"ALEXEI!" squealed Kat and ran after him.

"WAIT," yelled Nikolai and set off in pursuit of Kat.

A white flash zipped past Kat, then another. In a moment they were swallowed by the night. She stopped and Nikolai ran into her back. They tumbled to the ground, their torches somersaulting after them.

There was enough of Johann Daniel's fire potion on each to ensure neither went out. Kat scrambled towards hers, grabbed it and raised it above her head.

"Whooossshh," went the steppe as enough of the potion fell from Nikolai's torch to set the grass alight. It spat and snapped in protest.

Nikolai seized his torch before it could be caught in the flames and stepped back alongside Kat.

"Alexei..." shouted Nikolai. "ALEXEI..."

The wind gusted from behind them pushing the fire away, which in turn blew away the darkness. The fire flared. Then began to die out. But in the brief lifting of the night's curtain, Kat and Nikolai caught sight of the old mare.

She was reared up, her front legs kicking out. In front of her two wolves shied out of reach of her hooves. She could do nothing about the two leaping through the air behind her, trying to join the one already on her back. The flicker of the flames, like a burst of lightening, caught the wolf's jaws open in the split second before it would force them onto the old mare's neck.

And behind them, also in mid-air, was Alexei, jumping for the old mare, fighting against the law of the Steppe; the law that says the weak will fall to the strong.

It was a fight even a fully grown giant could not have won. There was a howl as Alexei caught one of the wolves, both of them now in full flight. Alexei's weight took it and him away from the old mare and

123

they thrashed on the ground, a swirling mass of wolf and human.

Kat and Nikolai ran towards them waving their torches and yelling. The wolf snarled and snapped at Alexei, catching his arm and breaking free of his grip. It stood over him, close enough for Alexei to see into its yellow eyes. Alexei kicked out, catching the wolf on the head. It skidded back and then came again, fastening its jaws around his arm and shaking, trying to tear it off his body.

Alexei let out a yell of pain. Kat and Nikolai jumped together, their torches pointing at the wolf. Nikolai's poked into its side and it was the wolf's turn to let out a wounded yelp.

"Raaarrrrgggghhhh."

It was a roar of rage and it came from deep within Kat – she swung her torch against the wolf's skull, the beast's fur hissing as the fire singed it.

That was enough, the wolf sprung off and retreated to what it judged a safe distance. Alexei groaned. The wolf snarled and took a pace towards them. Kat and Nikolai reached for each other's free hand and held tight as they swung their torches in the wolf's direction.

It paced back and forth out of the torches' reach, studying them, a look that said 'I could attack you and probably kill you but you could hurt me before I do so.' It did a cunning calculation and decided it was not worth it. A lone wounded wolf does not survive long on the steppe..

If the children were spared the old mare was not. The wolf turned and was swallowed up by the dark. They did not hear another sound – the mare had bolted, running for her life and a wolf pack does not howl during a hunt. It makes no sound at all, saving every single bit of energy for the hunt, and the kill.

Where exactly they caught the mare, Kat, Nikolai and Alexei never found out. There was no sign of her nor the wolf pack, and they never saw any sign of either again.

They helped Alexei up and tried their best to support him back to the carriage, but a girl with a crooked back and a dwarf are not designed to support a giant so it was an awkward and uncomfortable stagger back.

"We're going the wrong way," groaned Alexei.

"How do you know?" asked Kat. "It's dark, we can hardly see beyond our own footsteps."

"The breeze… it should be in our faces, it's in my left ear at the moment."

Daylight was breaking across the steppe by the time they reached the carriage.

15

"Jjjjaaaarrrrgggggghhhh."

Alexei's cry galloped across the steppe.

"For a boy who was going to be the Tzar's bodyguard you're as delicate as the Tzarina's pinky."

They had to clean his wound. The wolf had left its calling card down Alexei's big right arm, from the elbow to just above the wrist. The top part looked like two rows of sharp nails had been hammered into his arm and taken out again. The rest of it was marked by a deep cut. Johann Daniel had told Kat of the importance of keeping any wounds they suffered as clean as possible. If it wasn't cleaned, infection could set in and Alexei might lose his arm.

"And what use is a one-armed giant to anyone?"

pointed out Nikolai handing Alexei a piece of wood to bite on while Kat did the cleaning.

Next Kat used what was left of Olga's poultice. Nikolai had gasped when he'd peeled it off Kat a couple of days earlier – her cut had healed leaving barely a mark. Kat poured a little of their precious water on to the remaining poultice and smeared it onto the wound. She used what was left of Alexei's right sleeve to bandage it up.

"There," she said and sat back. The sun felt warm on the back of her neck, it was a pleasant feeling but there was nothing pleasant about their predicament.

They were stuck in the middle of nowhere with little food and water. If they continued on foot, carrying what they could, they'd be wide open to a wolf attack come nightfall. If they barricaded themselves beneath the carriage and waited in the hope of someone coming along... what if nobody did? What if a Guards patrol did? What if anyone did? The reaction of Olga's villagers suggested whoever found them would not be happy to help.

They had to go on.

"Tomorrow," said Kat. "Rest today, tomorrow we walk."

"Where?" said Nikolai. Kat scowled at him. "I have to ask... I mean look where we are, you've no idea do you?"

"East," said Kat. "We keep going east."

"Until when?"

"Until we get home."

Nikolai shrugged. "Yeah, right... till we get home. Wherever that is... if it even exists..."

Kat ignored him.

"We'll get there – I know we will."

They spent a nervous night beneath the carriage, blocking themselves in with their baggage and deciding not to light the torches in order to save the fire for when they had to sleep out in the open. Kat and Nikolai took it in turns to keep an ear out, swapping the knife with each watch, while Alexei slept like his usual log. They heard nothing, not even Nikolai's keen ears could pick out a growl or howl near or far.

In the morning they divided up what they could carry. The remains of Johann Daniel's bundle, all the food and as much water as they could each manage. Kat shoved a red ballet shoe into each pocket of her trousers.

Alexei, refreshed by sleep and the effect of the poultice, reckoned they had enough food and water to survive a week if they were careful – and lucky. "But if we don't find somewhere after that," he said cheerfully, "we'll in time die of thirst. We shall die of thirst before we die of hunger."

"Well, that's comforting," said Nikolai, heaving his share onto his back. "Because I'd hate to starve to death." The water sloshed in his carrier as though teasing them with their fate.

Johann Daniel's bottles clinked encouragingly as Kat lifted her side pack over her shoulders. It felt heavy, pulling her to one side. She stood as straight as she could and angled the rolled map over the other shoulder, like a soldier positioning his gun ready to march. There was no way she was leaving Johann Daniel's precious map behind, even if out here on the steppe it seemed next to useless – the steppe was an empty space.

Between Moscow and the Urals there was little at all on the map. There was, appropriately, a snarling wolf. Not far from the wolf was an eagle and a little further on from the tip of the majestic bird's spread wing was one of those Russian onion-dome churches, sitting on its own out on the steppe.

You never know, thought Kat, they had come across wolves so if she kept an eye on the sky for an eagle they might yet reach the onion church soon after. If it existed. She crossed the first two fingers on each hand.

"Off we go," she sang out, forcing her voice to sound as bright as the morning.

They followed the rough track. "It must lead somewhere," suggested Kat. "I mean who makes a path to nowhere?"

"Russians, Russian lumpens," grumbled Nikolai.

Kat tutted.

"What?" said Nikolai.

"Nothing."

"No, go on… say it."

Kat sighed.

"Look," said Nikolai, waving his arm ahead of them. "We've got all day and it's not as if we're going anywhere."

He sniggered and winked up at Alexei, who pretended to ignore him.

"Huh," said Kat.

"What's up – cat got your tongue?" Nikolai sniggered again, pleased with his joke.

Kat whirled round and rammed her hands against her hips. She glared at Nikolai.

"For goodness sake... can't you, just once... just once look on the bright side, be positive about what we're doing – we rescued you, got you out of the palace. You'd probably be dead if it wasn't for us and all you can do is moan."

She spread her arms. "Look where we are – look what we're doing... we're free, freer than we've ever been, freer than anyone in the Kunstkamera."

She tilted her head back and looked into the sky, small squiggles of white clouds patterned the blue, going on and on to the horizon and beyond.

"Yeah," said Nikolai, stomping past, head down, thumbs dug beneath his shoulder straps to ease the pull of his pack, "free to die on our own and have our skeletons picked clean by the crows and foxes – if we've not already been eaten by a wolf."

"Oh damn you, Nikolai Nikolayevich, you can go to hell."

This time it was Kat's turn to stomp on, her pack beating against her side with each step she took.

For a time, they went on in single file, Alexei leading, whistling to himself as he wondered along like a Sunday afternoon stroll, followed by Kat, followed by Nikolai. Kat muttered to herself, cursing Nikolai, deciding one firm punch would teach him a lesson, send him sprawling then she'd offer him her hand to pull him back to his feet and he'd apologise.

"I won't you know," he said.

"Oh," said Kat. She hadn't noticed Nikolai quickening his pace to walk alongside her.

"I won't apologise for what I am."

"Oh," said Kat again, "but I didn't mean that, I wasn't…"

"I know; it's just you need to understand what it's like being a… a dwarf. You see we grow up fearing the worst – I've been laughed at for as long as I can remember. And knocked about for as long as I can remember. The Boyars' children, in the Palace, they see how their fathers treat us and copy them – so they chase us and fight us… not real fights because we don't dare fight back… if you hit a noble…"

He shook his head.

"Fear the worst, our elders tell us. And it becomes a way of life. You live scared. Scared every morning what the day will do to you, scared every night what the night will bring for you. But it also helps you see, because if you expect the worst… well, you know what I mean…"

Kat said nothing.

"I am glad to be here – I really am, Katinka, it's just… it's just so big, so vast and we're so small…" Nikolai looked skywards as he spoke. "Hey, look, look up there… what's that?"

Kat's eyes followed his finger up into the sky.

"Is that an eagle?"

"I don't know," she said.

"It's big," said Nikolai.

"Looks like an eagle," announced Alexei. He'd stopped and was shielding his eyes as he gazed up. The bird circled slowly, its wings spread. "Yes, that's an eagle."

"Hah!" said Kat, "just like the map says. We will get there I know it."

Nikolai opened his mouth. Then closed it. He swallowed the thought.

They walked into the day. It was not difficult walking. A little bit of up, a little bit of down and a lot of plodding. Their bags grew heavier as the day wore on, at least for Kat and Nikolai they did. Alexei strode ahead, taking one stride for every three or four of the others.

He looked taller out here, as if being freed from the Winter Palace and the cramped, crowded spaces of St Petersburg had given him a growth spurt. Kat watched him and wondered if fresh air, real fresh air you could taste, might make up for the lack of food.

"I'm hungry," declared Alexei.

They stopped for a time but having decided to save their food until evening there didn't seem much point so they took a swig of water and walked on. Nothing changed around them.

Kat had a blister on her left big toe. She found if she limped it didn't hurt as much. At last, with the sun waving so long to the day, Alexei dropped his pack to the ground. They were on the top of a small rise.

"Let's stay here for the night."

The next morning brought no change. They walked, Kat and Nikolai bickered, they sipped at their water and massaged sore feet, then they walked some more. The eagle reappeared in the late afternoon, and this time it swooped, diving out of the sky, talons outstretched. It caught something, a rabbit probably, and whatever it was managed to wriggle free.

"The fall will kill it," said Alexei. "Come on let's go and look for it."

He dropped his pack on the track and lolloped off across the grass.

"He's racing an eagle for a rabbit – he really is hungry," said Nikolai.

They watched the giant boy run across the steppe and the giant bird hover above, sharp eyes searching for the rabbit. It had done the hard work in catching its prey and wasn't going to let anyone spoil its dinner plans.

"He'll never do it," said Nikolai.

"I've never eaten rabbit," said Kat, rubbing her stomach. She reckoned she'd eat just about anything to avoid having to fall back on the grass porridge.

"RUN, ALEXEI, RUN," yelled Nikolai. He turned to Kat. "Come on, if we run after him waving our arms it might scare off the eagle."

"Us? Scare off an eagle?"

"Run," said Nikolai and set off.

Kat laid down the map carefully and lifted her pack over her shoulder. She felt light again as she dropped it to the ground, like when she danced, floating across the floor. She ran, dashing over the grass and soon overtook Nikolai.

They hared over the steppe behind Alexei, leaping and waving their arms. Alexei looked back as he ran and a huge grin split his big round face. That was a mistake – not the grin, the looking back because it meant he failed to spot a rock and seconds later that big round face slapped into the ground.

"ALEXEI!"

Kat's cry of alarm skipped ahead of her. But there was no need for it. A fall that might have knocked out an every-day sized boy left Alexei with a scratch down one side of his face and a mouthful of dust but otherwise no damage done. He was up again in a moment, scrabbling back to his feet and resuming the chase.

The three of them ran and laughed and yelled and hooted and screamed and leapt and whirled their arms around like windmills in a hurricane.

"There it is," roared Alexei.

The eagle looked on from above, and if eagles can be said to shrug, that's what it did. Time for a change of mind. It may have done the work in catching dinner but these three mad people below could keep it – he wasn't going near them. There were plenty more rabbits on the steppe. The eagle flapped its mighty wings and rose higher into the sky. Soon it was a dot, then it was gone.

16

Roast rabbit, so it turned out, cooked on a stick over a small fire with sizzling chunks torn off with sticky fingers was the nicest thing Kat had ever eaten. That's what it tasted like that night as they sat out on the steppe grinning at each other, blowing on hot fingers and chewing their first proper meal in days.

Kat used up the last of her fire-starting potion to light the fire and one final torch. There had been no discussion – the prospect of a hot dinner quelled any doubts.

"Ahhhh," sighed Nikolai and lay back in the grass. "Pinch me I must be dreaming."

"Owwww!" He leapt up. "Kat... what..."

"See," she said as Alexei let out a giant guffaw, "it's no dream."

"That hurt," mumbled Nikolai.

Alexei nudged him. "You ran like the wind over the steppe, my little friend."

"Did I?"

"Nikolai, the bird boy," said Kat. "You sing and you fly."

Nikolai lay back again, a contented smile across his face and a warm feeling in his stomach which wasn't only from having a full belly. Perhaps he should stop fearing the worst.

Kat unrolled the map and studied it by the flickering light of the fire.

"Look," she said stabbing a finger at it. "Wolf... eagle..."

She traced her finger on. "A dome... somewhere out there. We can find it, buy food and then..." her finger ran on... "the Urals."

She looked up at Alexei, her eyes glowing in the firelight. "The Urals."

Alexei shook his head. Nikolai sat up.

"Johann Daniel is guiding us," insisted Kat, nodding her head at Alexei.

Nikolai, his head nearly touching Kat's as he too peered down at the map, ran a finger of his own over its surface, tracing their route from St Petersburg to where the eagle's talons grasped... he lent closer: "A rabbit. That's a rabbit – look, it's got a rabbit and it's... look, it's offering it... offering it to us... it is, isn't it?"

Alexei shook his head again. Kat nodded hers.

"He is, isn't he? I knew it – I knew it, I told you didn't I – I did."

Alexei kept shaking his head.

"A wizard, Tzar Peter's wizard – we're being guided by Tzar Peter's wizard."

Alexei shrugged and lay down, resting his head on his pack. He closed his eyes.

"Wake me when it's my watch."

Nikolai shuffled close to Kat, together they leaned over the map.

"If we start early," whispered Kat, "set off at sun rise, then we should see the dome by sunset or maybe the next day."

"Tell me," said Nikolai, "is Johann Daniel hundreds of years old? He could be... all those wrinkles... his face looks like a map, doesn't it?"

"We should rest."

"You sleep; I'll take first watch."

Kat closed her eyes and sleep came to the accompaniment of Nikolai singing softly to himself. She didn't know the song, but the tune was a happy one. She liked hearing Nikolai sing, liked hearing him happy. Happiness was catching.

It took until the following afternoon for the good mood to scatter across the steppe. There was no change, rolling grasslands in every direction. Their water was almost gone – they didn't have enough to make it worth boiling up grass porridge. The torch was still alight, just. But it was unlikely to make it through the night.

It lasted until an hour, maybe two, after dark.

"Splut," it went and darkness folded around them.

Kat shivered. "Tomorrow," she said in as firm a voice as she could manage. "We will see the dome tomorrow. I promise."

She swallowed. Her throat was dry – they were saving the last swig of water for the morning. "I promise," she repeated, then dropped her voice. "Please, Johann Daniel, please."

She aimed her soft words into the night sky, hoping the breeze would take them and fly them back west, all the way to St Petersburg and the Winter Palace.

There they would find a way in through an open window – there was always one – and into the room with the dome where a cloaked figure would be bent over a book or a parchment.

Kat sighed and the breeze took that as well.

* * *

Because Alexei was the tallest, he saw it first. They'd reached the top of a rise, one of the bigger ones they'd trudged up since leaving the forest days ago (even Kat was no longer sure how many days – there didn't seem any point in counting).

"There," he said and pointed. He held his arm up for a moment longer, then let it drop.

"What?" asked Kat.

"Can't see anything," stated Nikolai.

Alexei spun round and grabbed Nikolai under the armpits. With one grunt he hoicked him over his head and plonked him on his shoulders, like a father lifting his young son up for a better view.

"What is it, Nikolai? What can you see?"

Nikolai's mouth dropped open. For quite possibly the first time in his life he was lost for words.

"It's... it's..."

143

"A dome," said Alexei, swinging Nikolai back to the ground. "A golden dome."

Nikolai's mouth was opening and closing like a freshly-caught fish but still nothing came out.

Kat stood on her tiptoes. She couldn't see it.

"How far?"

Alexei shrugged. "Not far – we'll be there before nightfall."

"The map..." Kat looked up at Alexei. "Johann Daniel... how did he know?"

Alexei shrugged again.

"Wizard," said Nikolai, at last stopping the word whizzing round his brain and getting it out his mouth. "The Tzar's wizard."

17

They reached the monastery as the sun set. The dome crowned a tall whitewashed tower. Beneath it a large wooden door was shut tight. Within it was a smaller door, the size of a man. The monastery was a square building, the front built of stone and whitewashed like the tower. As they walked down towards it, they could see the other three sides were less impressive, built of stacked logs.

A cluster of huts sat before the monastery and beyond them a chunk of steppe was ploughed into three large fields. A fence tracked around another mouthful of land and in it several horses grazed.

"Let's use Johann Daniel's coins and buy horses

– then we'll be in the Urals in no time," suggested Nikolai. "We'll need a big one for you Alexei but me and Kat we can get ponies."

Eying up the monastery as they approached its huge gates, Kat felt anxious. She stopped and rummaged in her pack, found the coin pouch. She slipped off her cloak and pulled down her right sleeve so she could slide the pouch's drawstring up her arm. The pouch hung in her armpit.

She bent down again and reached for the last two of Johann Daniel's small bottles then hesitated. She thought for a moment and decided to leave them in her pack.

When the track reached the turning to the monastery, Kat asked the other two to wait. She clambered over the small ditch running along one side and disappeared behind a bush.

She wasn't sure why she did what she did – hiding the coins on her, not hiding the bottles and now hiding the map (along with her precious red ballet shoes) – but something was telling her to. Or someone.

Little is what it first seems in Russia. Like Johann Daniel's map. If you studied it extra carefully, as Kat had, and paid particular attention to the drawing of the onion-domed tower they now appeared to be approaching, then it was possible to make out a small skull and crossbones drawn in one of the tower's tiny windows and at the foot of the tower sat a small cat.

She remembered one evening back in the Winter Palace when she'd been called to see Johann Daniel in the library. It was a few nights after she'd been whipped by Prince Sikorsky's man. The Prince had watched and counted off the strokes with a tap of his foot and a look of mounting fury at her refusal to cry out.

When it was done he bent over her as she lay on the floor, biting her lip in determination not to let him see her pain. "If I see you again out of the Tzar's sight, I will kill you myself," he whispered in her ear. "Remember this palace is full of dark corners and I know them all."

She was about to open the library door when she noticed a scrap of paper pushed underneath. On it was a hurried sketch, a cat sitting above a skull and cross bones. Footsteps approached the other side of the door. She pressed herself into an alcove.

She didn't see him but she heard his voice, the distinctive high-pitched whine of Prince Sikorsky. "See to it at once, man, or you will suffer."

She listened to the click of his boots taking him down the corridor and away. She let out a long breath.

"Clever Koshka." She smiled at the voice coming from the library. Koshka, cat – his special name for her because she was so light on her feet. "Come in, my dear – the coast's clear." Johann Daniel was her protector, if she didn't know it then, she did now.

Kat didn't tell the boys what she'd done with the map, or what she had spotted on it. They thought she nipped behind the bush for something else entirely. She didn't want to spoil their mood – Nikolai was the happiest she'd seen him. Even Alexei appeared, by his careful standards, satisfied.

Alexei banged on the door-within-a-door. Nothing happened. Silence settled again on the valley.

"It's all so quiet," said Kat looking behind as if worried someone might be creeping up on them.

Alexei banged again, this time louder. A panel in the door-within-a-door opened suddenly enough to make them jump.

A bearded face stared fiercely at them.

"Please can you help us, my lord," said Kat, her voice as sweet and sing-songy as she could make it. "We've travelled many versts on our long journey home and we are in desperate need of food and shelter."

The man said nothing.

"Just for one night, please my lord monk."

The panel slammed shut.

"My lord monk!" Nikolai shook his head. "What a load of…"

Nikolai was interrupted by the door-within-a-door opening. It creaked a protest as if it had been a while since it had last been used.

The monk, who wore a long black robe covering him from neck to toe, gestured for them to follow.

The door opened into an archway. A thick bell rope dangled from a round hole at the height of the arch. The archway itself led to a cobbled courtyard but the monk turned into the stone building and up a narrow flight of stairs that curved through the tower. The only sound was the slap of footsteps on the stone stairs.

"Thank you for taking us in," said Kat, hurrying to

keep up with the monk's brisk pace. "It's terribly kind of you."

The monk said nothing. Instead he paused outside another door and pointed at it.

"We're to go in there?"

He nodded and Kat opened the door and led the boys into a large room with an appropriately-sized fireplace filling most of the far end.

The door slammed behind them. The monk had not followed them in.

The children looked around. Rough wooden benches and a long table ran down one side, beneath a row of square windows cut into the wall at head height (or chest height if you were Alexei). The room was gloomy and needed the fire for light as much as heat. Around the fire was a semi-circle of wooden chairs. They could see the tops of heads peeking over the backs of the chairs. There seemed to be no interest in their arrival.

"Hello, your highnesses," said Kat. "You are so very kind to take us in for the night – and it will be just the one night, that I promise on the Holy Mother herself."

A monk who looked as old as earth itself stood up

and stepped from his chair to face them. His beard was white and came down to his waist.

He raised an angry finger at them, and then lifted it to his lips.

"I'm sorry, I didn't mean to disturb you – I hope we didn't wake you."

The old monk raised his finger again and repeated his action.

"I…" began Kat as the door opened again.

"He won't answer you."

The three of them spun round. A tall, slightly stooped man stood there smiling. He also wore a long robe but his was white and around his neck hung a heavy gold chain. On his head was a high rectangular hat, also white, with a golden cross marked on the front.

"Why not?"

"Nobody within these walls will."

"Apart from you," pointed out Nikolai.

The smile disappeared from the man's face only to return a moment later.

"Ah yes, apart from me. You see this is a silent order – we do not speak. We have taken a vow of silence in order to serve our Lord and Master."

"Apart from you," pointed out Nikolai.

"I," said the man, trying to contain his irritation with Nikolai, "am the Starets, appointed by St Abraham of Smolensk himself. I am the sole man allowed to speak within these walls. This is my monastery."

"That must be good," said Nikolai.

"What?" snapped the Starets.

"Being the only one allowed to talk – bet you'd like that Kat. You wouldn't have to put up with me questioning your ideas all the time would you. It was her idea, you see your High Staretsness, to follow the map and…"

"SILENCE."

Kat's bad feeling began to grow.

"Who are you, you… you three…"

"You see, sir, we're travelling to find my mother and father, looking for my home and we just needed…"

The Starets was shaking his head. "No," he said. "I will not have it, we are a house of God – we live on God's land, we cannot have people like… like you… insults to His creation…" his lip curled as he spoke "… wandering across my estate."

He clapped his hands twice and the monks seated around the fire rose together. There was a dozen of them; all, apart from the old man who'd tried to hush Kat, broad and strong. Daggers hung from cords wrapped around their robes.

"Fetch the watch," said the Starets. "At once."

One of the monks hurried off.

"Your Highness," began Kat, "we only…"

"I said silence," hissed the Starets. "I am the only one to speak within these walls. You will not speak to me unless I say you can. If you break my command, you will be flogged."

The door opened once more and another six monks, brandishing wooden clubs, entered.

"Take them to the cells – bring me their bags. If you hear one word from them… where is Monk Artemis?"

One of the club monks pointed to the door as another monk ducked through it and he needed to duck because he was immense – the huge gates to the monastery might have been carved just for him. He made Alexei look the size of Nikolai.

"Lock them up, Monk Artemis."

Artemis nodded and gestured at the children. He let out a low growl.

"Is that allowed?" said Nikolai and grinned at the others. But inside he was cursing himself. Why, he thought, did I ever think to stop fearing the worst?

18

"They'll kill us, I know they will – they're no different to the Boyars at the Palace, they're monsters… monsters. It doesn't matter where we go, lumpens will always drive us out – if they don't kill us first. I'm going to die in a monastery in the middle of nowhere and no-one will know I'm gone and no-one will care…"

"Nikolai, please… sit down."

Nikolai reached the end of the cell and took seven paces back to the door, turned and took seven paces back to the wall stepping over Alexei's legs as he went. Kat sat next to Alexei, hugging her legs to herself.

"We should have stayed in St Petersburg… at least I knew where to hide in St Petersburg… and we got fed and I knew… I knew…"

"Nikolai... Nikolai..." Kat stood up and blocked his way.

"What?" he said. "No, no... you got us into this... this nightmare, locked up by hairy, mute monks. Can you get us out of it? No, of course you can't. Now, get out of my way – I want to pace."

Kat sat down again. "I think I can."

Her voice was little more than a whisper.

"What?" Nikolai turned sharply by the door. Alexei looked up.

"Can you?" said the giant.

"It might not work," said Kat.

"Oh, what a surprise," said Nikolai and resumed pacing. "I wonder how they'll kill us... I've heard monks can be even crueller than the Boyars... oh, this is going to be a sticky end..."

"Listen," said Kat, "carefully."

Nikolai shrugged. "Oh, well I suppose we might as well go down with a fight."

He sat down opposite Kat. She fixed stubborn eyes on him. "Yes, I got us into this and I will get you out – I promise."

"Huh," said Nikolai, but he listened intently, his head cocked to one side as Kat revealed her plan.

She spoke for several minutes and when she finished Alexei nodded.

"Yes," he said, reaching out and taking Kat's hand – it disappeared inside his. "I understand, little sister."

"Huh," said Nikolai. "Lot of ifs in there."

*   *   *

Nikolai may have feared the worst but it didn't mean he wouldn't try his hardest to stop the worst happening.

He and Alexei sat in silence when Monk Artemis came for Kat that night – just as she said he would. Their part would come later.

There was no rattle of a key or clunk of a bolt being drawn, the door just opened and there he was, pointing at her and flicking his head for her to follow him. A deathly quiet hung over the entire place, as if the huge doors blocked all sound.

Kat swallowed as Artemis led her up the winding stairs and back to the hall where the Starets waited.

He was sitting at the far end of the long table, two small bottles, one blue, one green, in front of him. A candle flickered on the table. Artemis gave her a shove into the room.

"Leave us Monk Artemis," said the Starets. "I think I can handle a hunchback without your help."

He smiled at Kat as he spoke. It made her flesh crawl.

"Stand there," he said, indicating a spot in front of the table with a flick of a long finger. Kat noticed the large gold ring on it and checked a smile.

"These," said the Starets, "these bottles in your bag, what are they?"

Kat shrugged. Don't make it easy, she reminded herself, nothing comes easy in Russia.

"I said: what are they?"

She shook her head.

"Ah," said the Starets, "I see… playing clever are we."

He stood up, the chair scraping on the floor. Its harsh noise, unexpected in this house of silence, made Kat start. She could feel the tension flooding through her. Breathe, she thought, breathe.

The Starets walked behind her. She felt his hot breath on her neck. It smelt of onions and wine. She wrinkled her nose. She felt his bony fingers grip her shoulder. They dug in and she flinched.

"I can play clever too, you little freak." He whispered in her ear.

"Now," he said, returning to his chair and smiling at her. "This one, this blue bottle, what's in here?"

"It's for cooking, that's all."

"For cooking?"

"Yes, cooking, it's herbs and spices, dried and ground – makes plain food taste nice."

The Starets studied her. "I can tell a liar a mile off," he said. "Herbs and spices you say?"

"Yes, smell them if you don't believe me."

"Believe you? Why would I believe a word that crosses your disgusting lips."

Kat shrugged again. She noticed two large gold rings on his other hand.

"I can have it whipped out of you – Monk Artemis is skilled with the whip. It wouldn't take long for you to start singing."

Kat squeezed her eyes shut and sniffed. She opened them again and forced a tear down her left cheek.

"Sir, it is for cooking, herbs and spices I promise you – I swear, I swear on, on…"

"Your life?"

She nodded.

"Well, your life's not worth very much."

Another tear tracked its way down her face.

"Herbs and spices, sir."

With a twist of his fingers he popped the stopper from the bottle and held it at a distance. Carefully he moved it towards his face and then his nose. He sniffed loudly.

"Herbs and spices," he said and replaced the stopper. He picked up the green bottle and studied it. "But it's this one, this is the one that interests me."

The Starets sat up, narrowed his eyes and studied Kat. "Where have you come from? Where did you get these?"

Kat shifted her eyes around the room, darting them from the door to the windows to the fireplace to the table. She looked everywhere but at the Starets.

"Shall I have you whipped, girl? Shall I have your little friend thrown to the dogs? The big one chopped up? One of you will talk, I don't care which one."

"Sir… no, sir, please sir…"

"Yes?"

"Sir, we ran away, sir."

Kat's tears were flowing freely now. She sniffed and wiped her nose.

"Go on."

"From the palace, the Tzar's Palace."

"The Winter Palace?"

"Sir, yes, sir."

"You're lying."

"No, sir, I belonged to the Tzar's physician you see, fetched and carried and cleaned in his rooms. He made magic – I saw it. I did, sir."

"Magic? What are you talking about?"

"Gold, sir, I saw it with my own eyes – he made gold… using that." She pointed at the green bottle he held in his right hand.

"Can you read?"

"Me, sir, no sir – reading's for proper people, not the likes of me, sir."

"Well quite." He turned the bottle round so the label was facing Kat.

"What does that say?"

"Gold, sir?"

"No, you can't read can you – it says 'Alchemy'. Do you know what alchemy is?"

"No, sir."

"Making metal into gold, that's what alchemy is… hmmmm…"

The Starets stood up again and circled behind Kat. He moved without sound.

"You saw it happen? You watched the Tzar's physician turn base metal into pure gold?"

Kat nodded.

"Then you and your freak friends stole his potion and ran away, thinking you could make your fortune eh?"

Kat bit her lip and sniffed.

"No, sir, we didn't, we…"

"You stole it." The Starets was standing behind her again. "You know what happens to thieves, don't you, girl?"

"We didn't, sir, we didn't…"

The Starets tutted and returned to his seat. He picked up the bottle, stared at it for a while, silence settling on the room. Kat could feel her heart pounding. This was the moment.

"You can show me?"

Kat nodded, still chewing her bottom lip.

"Show me how to turn metal into gold."

She could see the gleam in his eye. Pure greed.

She nodded. He leaned forward.

"I will spare you if you show me…"

"And my friends…"

He nodded this time, and pointed at her. The golden ring on his finger glinted in the candle light. "But you listen to me, you little witch, any funny business and Monk Artemis will cut the heads off all three of you and yours will be the last head to fall."

Kat swallowed hard. This was going to work – just so long as Alexei and Nikolai followed their part of the plan. If they couldn't then she was going to lose her head.

19

"Pssssssst."

The stone floor was cold against Nikolai's cheek. He pushed his face harder against the bottom of the cell door and tried again.

"Psssssssssssssst."

Footsteps, coming his way. He listened: only one set. Perfect.

"Pssssssssssssssssssssssst."

He slid the gold coin under the door and listened to it scrape across the corridor. He pressed his lips almost beneath the door.

"Listen to me – I've plenty more where that came from. St Petersburg gold – help me and it's all yours."

He heard the coin being picked up.

"Shhhh – ha! I don't need to tell you to keep quiet do I... the big one, he's asleep so I need to be quiet. Let me out and I'll give you the rest of this coin pouch..."

He jiggled it so the coins clinked together, the greatest sound in the world for a greedy man. An eye appeared at the peephole. Nikolai raised the pouch then pressed a finger to his lips and pointed at Alexei, who lay on the floor facing the wall. He let out a loud snore – careful, thought Nikolai, don't overdo it, you big ox.

The eye disappeared. "Come on, come on, you're a greedy lumpen – you can't resist," whispered Nikolai.

Nikolai counted one, two, three, four, fi... and the door slowly opened. "Got him," whispered Nikolai.

"Gold," he said, holding up the bag. "All gold."

The monk hesitated in the doorway, a club clutched in one hand. He knew it was too good to be true. Nikolai crouched, opened the pouch and counted out the gold coins into a small pile. Too good to be true, yes, but... but... this was a fortune, more gold than he'd ever seen.

The monk looked at Nikolai, who lowered his voice. "Let me out of here and out of the monastery. Is there a back way out?"

The monk nodded.

"Where?"

The monk jerked his hand this way and that, handing out directions.

"That near the stables?"

The monk nodded again. It was Alexei who said they would bring the horses into the monastery at night – they were too valuable to leave outside the walls.

"I give you half now, the rest when I'm outside."

The monk shook his head and put his hand out. Of course, thought Nikolai, you have no intention of letting me out, you just want the gold.

Nikolai gathered up the coins and stepped back, deeper into the cell. Now he shook his head.

"We have a deal, brother?"

The monk stepped into the cell and raised his club. Nikolai gave a quiet yelp and pressed himself into the empty corner. The monk grinned, his focus all on Nikolai and the pouch he held in his left hand. Nikolai put it behind his back.

"You m-m-m-ust help me," he said, adding a quaver to his voice. "Dumb lumpen."

The monk looked puzzled but only for a moment because it was in that moment Alexei came alive. He swept his legs across the floor, tripping the monk and sending him crashing to the ground.

"Oooooooooffff," he said as he hit it.

"Now, now," said Nikolai, as he leapt on top of the grounded monk and yanked his hood up over his head, "vow of silence, remember."

They tied up the monk, tearing a piece of cloth off his cloak and stuffing it in his mouth just in case he was tempted to break his vow, and peeked into the corridor. There was nobody in sight.

At the top of the stairs they split up. "Good luck, Alexei," said Nikolai. Alexei nodded at him.

Hoping the monk had been telling the truth about the location of the stables, Nikolai headed off to find three horses, saddle them and get them outside the main gate to wait for the others. If they didn't come, he was to ride off on his own – when Kat outlined that bit of the plan he refused.

"I will come and find you."

"No," she insisted, "if we don't come out it's because

we've failed – you won't be able to do anything for us... except save yourself, Nikolai."

He still wasn't sure what to do if they didn't turn up. He crossed his fingers as he scuttled across the courtyard, hopefully it wouldn't come to that. He could smell the horses – was this actually going to work? If, if, if... there were still too many for his liking. He slipped into the first stall and clucked softly at the small horse that faced him. There was no way he was going to be the one to mess it up.

*   *   *

Kat could see through the Starets' eyes the battle inside his head. He was a suspicious man and a greedy man, and Kat had a pretty good idea which side would win. The rings on his fingers and the necklace that kept catching the candles' rays gave a clue.

A gleam came into those give-away eyes as he watched her set up the bits and pieces she said they needed to perform alchemy.

"We must be careful," she said. "It's a very delicate matter, there's much that can go wrong."

"Yes, yes," said the Starets, "get on with it, girl."

He'd ordered Artemis to collect the pots and pans Kat required. A burner, normally used in the monastery's church, had been pressed into service as well as a length of pipe. Kat demanded it be cut in two. She then rejected the first two pieces of metal Artemis brought to be turned into gold.

The Starets studied her, suspicion filtering into his eyes, but greed drove it out.

"Do as she says," he instructed.

"Oh and I need one of those things you turn over and sand runs out."

"What?"

"You know, the sands of time, one of those."

"An hourglass?"

"Yes, that."

The Starets sighed. "Yes, all right... Artemis fetch her an hourglass as well."

It gave Kat a little longer to work out exactly what she was going to do – after all she was making up an experiment to turn metal into gold. It had to look good. And it gave Alexei and Nikolai as long as possible to complete their side of the plan.

"Yes," she said when Artemis returned with a small knife and an hourglass, "perfect."

She lit the burner, placed the knife flat in a frying pan and held it over the flame.

"It takes a little bit of time," she said, "this has to heat up."

They waited. "How long?" said the Starets. He was impatient.

"Soon – when half the sand runs through the timer," said Kat, turning it over. "Here you hold it."

She offered the pan handle to Artemis, who took it. Kat picked up the two pieces of pipe and fussed over them and the other pots and pans, muttering instructions to herself.

"It's through, the sand's through – do it," barked the Starets, eyes lighting up.

"Here goes," said Kat, picking up the Alchemy bottle. "Lean close – you must watch this; it is a wonder of the world."

She pulled out the stopper and carefully poured a couple of drops on to the knife, then a couple more.

The Starets and Artemis lent over the pan. The syrupy green liquid fizzed as it met the heat. A waft of smoke puffed into their faces. A strange smell followed close behind. The Starets coughed.

"Watch," said Kat, "you'll see it start to change in a moment, watch closely."

She could feel her eyes smarting. She hoped she'd put the right amount on. "A matter of drops, that's all," Johann Daniel had instructed. "Too much and… well, just do not put too much on or you might never wake up."

The smell grew stronger and another puff of smoke filled their faces.

The Starets coughed again. "What… what…" he said but got no further with his question. A puzzled expression crossed Artemis' face as he watched the Starets slither to the floor.

There was a crash as Artemis dropped the pot. It fell on to the burner and knocked it over. The oil spread across the table, the flame hurrying after it. Artemis blinked in surprise and then his legs stopped working as well.

Kat was the last to go because she had stepped away from the pan, but it took her too. The sleeping potion did not take long to work and soon she was on the floor with the two monks, although not before her brain had sent a desperate signal to her body about the fire taking hold on the table.

It was too late. "Ahhhh," sighed Kat and her eyes shut, ignoring the urgent message coming from her brain.

20

Alexei stopped and listened at the top of the stairs. Not a sound. He shuddered. This place gave him the creeps. It felt bad.

He shook his head, trying to clear it. It smelt odd too. He sniffed the air. There was a strange aroma in the corridor outside the hall. It must be the potion Kat was using, the Emergency Trick given her by Johann Daniel just in case. His job was to carry off the sleeping Kat and find Nikolai and the horses.

Kat had suggested he wait before coming in, in case the potion put him to sleep as well. That would be a spectacular fail.

He sniffed again. There was something else. It wasn't only his sense of smell telling him something was wrong. He could feel it. He approached the door and pressed his ear to it. It was hot. A whisper of smoke sneaked beneath it.

"Katinka!" yelled Alexei and opened the door.

The flames cackled a greeting. They had first lit up the table then moved on hungrily. There was plenty in the room to feed on. Some of the long curtains covering the windows were alight. Even a few of the wooden supports up in the roof were already on fire.

"Kat!"

Alexei scanned the smoky room. Three clothed heaps lay close to the table, one smaller than the others.

"Kat…"

Alexei leapt over to her, lifted her by the shoulders and shook her.

"Kat… no…"

The smoke caught his open mouth and he coughed. It was difficult to breath. He ran back to the door. The smoke was taking over the corridor too but he was able to snatch a deep breath. His head cleared – of course Kat was unconscious, it was the potion. But it would soon be the smoke, and then the flames.

He covered his mouth with his arm as he ran back to her, then clamped it shut as he bent and scooped her into his arms. She was light as a summer's morning. Her head lolled back. He carried her over to one of the windows and shoved it open. A gust of wind encouraged another delighted cackle from the rising fire.

He wrapped her in the curtain, one not yet claimed by the fire, and tied her tight. Only her face was visible. She looked like a baby swaddled by her mother. Her face was calm, no frowns or signs of pain or anxiety at what was going on around her. It was as though her unconscious mind knew she could trust Alexei.

Carefully he eased her out of the window and lowered her down as far as the curtain would allow. A surge of relief lifted him as he she stopped just about within reach of the ground, certainly in reach of someone tall on horseback. Like a young giant.

Back in the room he grabbed the Starets by his legs and dragged him into the corridor. He stared back into the hall. The fire had taken control and as if to show off its grip a burning rafter came crashing down.

Alexei could no longer see Artemis. But he wasn't going to leave him. The boy took a deep breath and edged past the rafter, keeping an eye on the roof in case any more came down.

He heard a cough and through the thickening smoke caught sight of Artemis. The huge monk was sitting up, too dazed to do anything more than stare at the inferno rising around him.

"You?" he grunted as Alexei wrapped an arm around his big shoulders and heaved him onto unsteady feet.

"You shouldn't be talking," muttered Alexei as he half carried, half dragged Artemis out into the corridor.

He dropped him alongside the still unmoving Starets and pulled the door to the hall closed. Time to find Nikolai and get away. As he passed the two men on the floor a hand caught his ankle.

Alexei pulled hard and the grip loosened. He looked down. It was Artemis, his face blackened with soot.

"Why?" he croaked.

Alexei pulled again and the fingers released their hold. He headed down the corridor without a backward glance and raced down the stairs. There was still not a soul in sight – the monks remained asleep

176

in their beds. In the archway Alexei leapt onto the bell rope and pulled, once, twice, three times and was answered by a deep clang from far above.

"What... you... eh?" The nightwatch-monk stumbled blearily out of the door on the other side of the arch, club in hand.

"Quick open the gates – get the serfs... fire... fire in the great hall... the Starets... help me, quick."

Alexei might have been able to shift the hefty wooden bar that secured the gates on his own, but not in a hurry and there was no time to lose.

"Stay here," ordered the monk as the gates began to creak open.

"No," said Alexei and swung his fist. The monk crumpled to the floor. "Sorry," said Alexei.

He gave the rope a couple of last heaves, prompting one more alarmed clang from the bell, and just for good measure bellowed "FIRE" a couple of times, before slipping through the gates. He shouldered them shut behind him – best not to make it obvious they'd got away quite yet.

He grinned as the gates clunked together. He glanced to his left then his right and the grin slid from his face. There was no sign of Nikolai.

"Nikolai?" he hissed. "Nikolai…"

Away to his right beneath the monastery's great hall a line of flame was sliding down a curtain that had escaped through one of the windows.

"Kat…"

He ran for her life. If the fire reached her first, unconscious and wrapped in the curtain, she would stand no chance.

The fire was raging. The precious glass in the windows shattered and the flames darted out into the night.

"ALEXEI!"

Nikolai was half lit by the flames. A small figure swaying as he tried to stand on a horse far too big for him, all the while clutching on to the reins of two ponies.

"I CAN'T REACH HER… I CAN'T REACH…"

Nikolai slithered to the ground as Alexei arrived. He held the reins while the giant mounted the horse.

Alexei stretched and his fingers brushed the fringe of the curtain. He couldn't get a hold on it. He looked up at the descending flames and cursed himself. Why hadn't he carried her out of the hall, left Artemis and the Starets, two men who would happily have let him burn, and taken her?

He needed to stand on the horse's back. He lifted his legs, crouched on the saddle and spread his arms to balance himself as he rose.

He was right to save the Starets and Artemis – you couldn't leave someone to die could you? It doesn't matter who they are. And if you leave them to die doesn't that make you like them? I'm not going to be like them – Alexei's brain was bouncing thoughts around his head. I'm going to be better than them, than those Boyars and all the hangers-on in the Winter Palace.

And I'm going to help Kat get what she wants, help her find her mother and father, help her find home. She's precious; I'm going to save her. He stood up and his head knocked against Kat's back. The curtain swung one way, taking her with it. He swung the other, flapping his arms like a baby bird trying to fly for the first time.

But he wasn't a baby bird, he was a young giant and young giants are not made to fly. He lost his footing and fell, thudding to the ground.

"ALEXEI!"

179

The fall knocked the breath from him. He rolled onto his back and groaned. Nikolai looked down on him.

"You all right?"

Above his head Alexei saw the flames begin to lick around Kat.

"NOOOO..." He pushed Nikolai aside and scrambled back onto the horse. His head was spinning. He jumped, in that desperate moment it was all he could think to do, and grabbed at Kat, his long arms wrapping around her.

Then he was falling again, falling backwards, and this time Kat was coming with him. The burning curtain was no match for his strength and he ripped Kat away.

Once more he landed on the ground and the air was smashed from his body. Kat was light but still heavy enough to hurt him.

Nikolai was there in an instant, tearing the rest of the curtain from Kat. She spun away like a Persian princess rolled out of a flying carpet.

"Kat? Kat..."

Nikolai crouched over her. Sparks from the torn curtain rained down on them, as if the fire were angry at being denied its prey. He lent down and put his ear to her mouth.

"She's breathing… quick help me get her on the horse."

Alexei groaned.

"Come on, don't just lie there – help me…"

Alexei rolled on all fours and pushed himself to his feet. He swayed like he was back on the horse.

"Can you lift her – we have to get away?"

Alexei grunted. He picked Kat up and draped her over the horse. He clambered up behind her, held her in place with one hand and took the reins with the other.

Nikolai leapt onto one of the ponies, the other's reins in his free hand.

"Let's go," he said.

He flicked the reins and urged the pony forward. He glanced back at Alexei.

"Ride, Alexei," he said. "Ride like the wind."

21

It was a good plan; a dangerous plan but a good one. They all agreed on that. Because if they'd not escaped... that didn't bear thinking about. Nevertheless, Kat felt guilty about the monastery going up in flames. They could still see the smoke rising above the steppe from many versts away, a dark smudge in the distance.

"Don't worry about it," said Nikolai. "Keeps them busy – less chance of them coming after us."

"Suppose," said Kat. Her head was throbbing and her throat felt like she'd gargled sand. She looked back at Alexei. His face was smeared black from the soot, his hair stuck out this way and that. He was riding with his eyes shut.

"Alexei?"

He opened them.

"Thank you."

He smiled a tired smile and closed his eyes once more.

Kat shifted in her saddle. She'd never ridden before and she wasn't entirely sure she liked it. Her and Nikolai were mounted on Siberian ponies, tough, broad-backed animals with spiky manes and dark eyes that made them look permanently cross. They stomped across the steppe, taking several steps for each one of Alexei's horse.

Kat had woken after they'd been in the saddle for a couple of hours. At first she hadn't a clue where she was, lying over Alexei's horse, hair hanging over her face. For a moment she thought she might be dead and being taken to the underworld.

They stopped at a stream and she dunked her entire head in it, feeling the freezing water jolt her back to life. She swallowed mouthful after mouthful but still her throat hurt and still she had a nagging thirst.

But she was alive – they were all alive and getting ever closer to the Urals. If the map was anything to go by they were perhaps only a couple of days ride away.

She smiled as she touched the map, rolled up and laid across the saddle in front of her, rather like she had been on Alexei's horse.

Nikolai was riding ahead of her, his little legs spread across the pony's stout back. She aimed her smile at Nikolai's back. It was he who had leapt from his pony and picked up the map and her ballet slippers from the bush where she'd hidden them.

"How did you know?" she asked.

He winked at her. "I see everything, Kat – that's how I survive."

They rode hard and left the monastery far behind, far enough to stop that night and sleep for a few hours. They were exhausted which at least distracted them from moaning bellies, grumbling at their emptiness.

Kat woke first. She rubbed her belly. She wished she still had that other bottle Johann Daniel had given her – she would have happily wolfed down several bowlfuls of grass porridge.

At least they had the coins. She squeezed the pouch, back beneath her armpit, to reassure herself of its contents and felt the letter crinkle at her touch. She wondered why Johann Daniel had given her a letter. Maybe it contained a list of useful spells for sticky situations… she shook her head. She was turning into Nikolai – of course it didn't because Johann Daniel was not a wizard. At least she didn't think he was.

She ordered herself to do exactly as he asked, open the letter when they came to the Yegoshikha River. Not before. No matter how much she wanted to.

She shivered and rubbed her arms. The weather was changing, autumn was here, Russia's mighty winter gathering behind it.

Kat took the map and clambered up a hill rising above where they'd spent the night. The countryside was beginning to change too. The flat sweep of the steppe was behind them, ahead the foothills of the Urals.

She was breathing heavily – and warmed up – by the time she reached the top. She put down the map and stood with hands on her hips. In front of her was a valley. They would have to travel up and down its sides – the sun was rising ahead of her and that was the way they wanted to go.

Kat unrolled the map and crouched to study it. Keep going east until you see Bear Mountain, Johann Daniel had instructed. There was nothing marked on the map before the Urals. Kat bent closer, making

185

sure there wasn't something she might have missed, another of his clues or warnings. She knew she would never see him again, yet she felt he was watching over them. Somehow. She couldn't make sense of the feeling, but it was definitely there.

"Kat," said Nikolai and Kat leapt up.

"Oh…" she yelped. "A fright – I was versts away."

"I wish we were," said Nikolai. "It's Alexei – he needs to eat, he's getting weak."

Kat scanned the horizon.

"Oh…" Another yelp. "Look – you can see them, look."

She pointed. Nikolai shook his head.

"There," she said. "There… the mountains, the Urals – it's the Urals."

Nikolai narrowed his eyes and stared. In the far distance there was a dark blue point just visible beneath the rising sun.

"It's the sun, the sun's making you see things."

"It's the Urals, I know it is – a day or two and we'll be there."

She turned to him and took his hands.

"Just think Nikolai, a few days and we'll be home… home…"

"Your home," he said and pulled his hands away.

"Our home," she said, taking hold of them again. "I promise you."

"You make a lot of promises, Katinka Dashkova… for someone who has nothing."

"I've got you Nikolai, and Alexei – apart from my mother and father there is nobody I'd rather have."

"Huh," said Nikolai. "Well. If we don't get the big lump something to eat soon you won't have him."

"I will…" Whatever she was going to say was interrupted by the distant bark of an explosion.

They swung round, Kat letting go of one of Nikolai's hands but keeping hold of the other.

"Cannons," said Nikolai. "That sounded like a cannon. Didn't it?"

"Don't know," said Kat, dropping his other hand, turning and setting off back down the hill. "But it means people and people mean food, come on, let's get Alexei."

* * *

It was not cannons, although Nikolai was nearly right because the explosion was caused by gunpowder.

Kat, Alexei and Nikolai lay in a row, looking down

187

on another valley. It was Alexei who'd urged caution – Kat wanted to gallop straight over the hill to find the soldiers. Because they thought it was cannon fire, they presumed they'd stumbled upon one of the Tzar's famous regiments.

"There might be officers who've been at the Winter Palace – they might recognise us and then…"

"He's right," agreed Nikolai. "Those soldiers can be… well, they're soldiers aren't they?"

Below them a dark scar was scraped across the valley floor. The scar ran down the valley from the south east, heading north-west. The explosion had blown up a large boulder in the canal's way. An ant's column of men were carrying away the remains.

"It's the Great Canal," whispered Nikolai.

They were a good distance from the men below, but when you're spying it seems right to speak in hushed tones.

"What?" said Kat. Sometimes it annoyed her that Nikolai seemed to know so much about what the Tzar was planning across his great Empire – yet was still convinced Johann Daniel was a wizard.

They think you're nobody, Nikolai explained to Kat one night. Because you're nothing, they (They again, thought Kat, always Them) never watch what they say in front of you so you pick up all sorts.

"The Great Canal, one of the Tzar's plans to make Russia as great as he is. Or was... It starts somewhere important – can't remember where – and goes all the way to the sea... somewhere. It goes from here to there, what more do you need to know?"

He shrugged. "Never thought it'd be worth remembering... anyway at the time I was singing to the Tzar, he was in a foul mood and told me to sing something soothing. He said he wanted to see ships sail across the steppe – it's supposed to be deep enough to carry great ships."

"Doesn't look very deep," said Alexei.

"They're in chains – the people digging," said Kat.

"Prisoners of the Tzar – they work till they die. Could have been us – could still be us if we're not careful... come on, let's go."

"No, wait," said Kat. "We need food – there'll be a camp somewhere, there'll be a kitchen somewhere in the camp."

Nikolai sighed. The clinks and clunks of spades and pickaxes attacking the dark earth drifted up to them. She was right – they might not find anywhere else. But they couldn't just wander down and ask for supplies. If they did they would be swinging a pickaxe in the canal before you could say "Long live the Tzarina."

22

Finding the camp was easy enough, a dusty, sprawling mishmash of tents and rough shelters further down the empty canal.

The lucky prisoners slept beneath the shelters, although they would not provide much cover when winter arrived. The rest slept in the open. There was no fence or wall to contain them. At night guards patrolled the edge of the sleeping area but it would take no great effort for a prisoner to slip away into the darkness.

Except the prisoner would still have chains around his ankles and, if they did make good their escape, they'd find themselves, well, nowhere. Escape was pointless. Some still did because starving to death, dying of thirst, dying of cold or being torn to pieces by wolves while pretending you were free again seemed like a better idea than dropping dead in the hated canal.

The cooking area was on the other side of the camp. Large cauldrons steamed on top of fires. They could make out small loaves of black bread stacked on tables. A cook, red faced and round stomached, was carrying pots in and out of a large tent. A tall thin man in the uniform of the Guards chatted to him as he worked. Otherwise there was little sign of life.

"We should wait until dark and sneak in," said Nikolai.

Kat shook her head. "Look, there are only two men down there – now's the best time."

"There'll be more in the tents."

Alexei nodded in agreement with Nikolai. He was too tired to spare any words. Taking just a single step was becoming a real effort. He looked down on the camp and saw a blur, his head felt as empty as his stomach.

"Not as many as there will be tonight when they're all back from working on the canal – we go now, we must," insisted Kat.

Nikolai scanned the other tents and returned his gaze to the kitchen area. He watched for a time.

"We must go now," repeated Kat.

"Wait."

"But…"

"Wait," repeated Nikolai. "For once in your life wait. Yes, we'll go soon, but first we must wait and watch, work out the best way."

Kat snorted her impatience. Nikolai ignored her and ran a careful eye over the camp. Alexei placed a large hand on Kat's shoulder.

"Wait," he grunted.

Kat forced a smile. He looked terrible, his face wolf white. She nodded.

After a time, Nikolai slid backwards and once hidden by the crest of the hill, stood up.

"It's time," he said.

They left Alexei – he was in no state to get involved – and coaxed their ponies down into the empty canal. This completed section was free of prisoners and guards and offered the perfect hidden path to the camp. "It's hardly deep enough to give Alexei a bath," remarked Nikolai.

It was deep enough to conceal their ponies. They

tethered them in the canal then climbed onto their backs to scramble out. They scampered up to the nearest tent and crouched outside, listening carefully. Not a sound.

Nikolai squirmed underneath the canvas and Kat followed. It smelt of unwashed bodies and dirty socks.

"Yuck," said Kat.

"Shhh," said Nikolai. He peeked through the flap at the front of the tent. There was no sign of anyone. The camp seemed to be taking an afternoon nap, enjoying the autumn sunshine, knowing there wasn't much of it left before the Winter Queen flew in from the east.

They worked their way from tent to tent towards the cooking area. Still not a sound. Until a gentle bubbling drifted from the cooking tent itself.

"He's boiling something – I'll have a look," cautioned Nikolai. He snuck his head round the opening to the huge kitchen tent. And giggled.

He waved a hand at Kat so she ducked her head round too, and pressed her hand over her mouth to stifle a giggle of her own.

The cook was asleep, sitting in a chair next to one

of the cauldrons, head tipped back, mouth hanging open. Steam rose from the cauldron; the loudest sound came from the cook. His snoring was like a bubbling pot, and between his snores he whistled like an impatient kettle.

Nikolai pointed at the tables and then at a pile of sacks beneath them. Kat nodded her understanding and slipped across the tent. She began to fill a sack with black bread. She hadn't been that bothered by hunger – she was used to going without – but now, handling food, she felt her pangs grow. She was starving.

She couldn't help herself, she broke off a chunk of bread and slipped it into her mouth, hoping Nikolai wouldn't notice. At once, in time with her first chew, she felt guilty. She tore off another piece, hissed and threw it over to Nikolai, who was standing guard by the sleeping cook, a large wooden spoon in one hand in case he should wake.

Kat munched happily on her mouthful, even if it was hard and bitter – prisoners' bread was as bad as you might expect. She filled the sack and added a handful of potatoes from the neighbouring table. It didn't sound much but rock bread and raw potatoes were going to seem a feast for Alexei – if they could get the food back to him.

The cook slept on. Nikolai stood on his tiptoes and looked into the cauldron. Whatever it was, some sort of soup or porridge – it was impossible to tell – it neither looked nor smelt good. In fact, thought Nikolai, it smelt like the foul air in the first tent they crawled into. Smelly feet soup, pong porridge… Nikolai grinned and Kat looked enquiringly at him.

He flicked his head. "Swap," he mouthed. Kat took the spoon and watched the snoring cook – each snore drew a stinking breath from within him and wafted it over her. She wrinkled her nose. She wished Nikolai would hurry up. This whole place was revolting. It stank of misery (and smelly feet) and she worried if they stayed too long the stench would stick to them.

"Let's go," said Nikolai at the exact moment the cook emitted such a loud snore he woke himself.

"Eh?" said the cook.

"Arrgghh," said Kat and without thinking walloped him on the head with the wooden spoon.

"Bok," said the spoon.

"Owwww," said the cook, trying to scramble

to his feet, hold his aching head, beat off Kat and work out what on earth was going on all at the same time.

"Run," barked Nikolai and Kat needed no second invitation.

The cook reached out a dirty hand for Kat but she skipped away and darted after Nikolai, who was already racing across the middle of the camp, his bread sack slung over one shoulder. There was no way he was leaving that behind. Alexei was depending on them and it felt good to be depended on.

Two things took Kat by surprise; firstly, she was laughing as she ran. The cook was bellowing behind her, she was running as fast as she could and she could hear herself laughing. They were going to get away with it. They always did. Everything they tried worked and that made her laugh, little old them, three Curiosities against Them. She and Nikolai were going to win again.

The second thing to take her by surprise was the guard, who threw her laugh away into the steppe sky as he crashed into her.

The sound of her laughter was replaced by a cry of pain as she hit the hard, dusty ground and the guard landed on top of her. She rolled to one side as his hands groped for her, their four legs flailing like young giraffes having their first neck fight.

Kat kicked out, connected only with fresh air, the guard rolled on top of her, pinning one arm to the ground. Out of the corner of her eye she saw Nikolai stop and turn back.

"Go," she yelled. "Go on…"

"Kat…"

"Goooo…"

The guard looked round, seeing who she was shouting at.

"He'll never get away," he snarled, which was a mistake as he should have been concentrating on stopping Kat rather than Nikolai.

With her free hand Kat scooped up a handful of dust and flung it into the guard's face. She followed it up by pinching his nose as hard as she could. When she thought back on the fight, it made her laugh – pinch his nose! What was she thinking about?

What was she thinking about? That's the thing about fighting for your life, you do the first thing that comes to mind, and sometimes before it even reaches your mind. You just do it.

The guard blinked furiously, his eyes stung, his vision blurred and his nose hurt like it had never hurt before. He let go of Kat's other arm and she took her chance to scoop another handful of dust into his face. She heaved at him and he toppled off her.

Kat leapt to her feet, grabbed her sack. Loaves tumbled out of it. She ignored them, swung what was left over her shoulder and took a step forward. It was only a step before she felt the sack nearly wrenched from her grasp.

The guard had hold of it. One glance told her if she wanted to keep the sack she would be caught. She let go and ran.

She was quick and had a start over the guard who was unsteady on his feet as he set off in pursuit. But he was a grown man, still young, well fed and certainly more recently fed than Kat. He was gaining on her, feet quickened by the desire for revenge on the girl with the crooked back who had humiliated a guard wearing the sacred uniform designed by the great Tzar himself.

Kat reached the canal. If she jumped into it he would catch her before she could get out the other side. She ran alongside the bank. He was catching her.

He was going to catch her, a few more strides and he would be able to grab her again. This time he would not fall for the dust in the eye trick.

"There's no getting away, freak." He spat the words at her back.

"KAT... KAT!"

"Nikolai!"

He was in the canal. His pony snorted, skittish, ready to run, sensing the need for flight. Nikolai held tight to the reins with one hand. In his other he held the reins to her pony. He pulled it alongside his and dug his heels into the flanks of his own. They moved level with her.

"JUMP," yelled Nikolai.

Kat shook her head and kept running.

"Yes... you can do it..."

The guard reached out and Kat felt his fingers brush her elbow, a few more strides and he'd have her. She was running out of breath, of time and even of belief. How could she ever dare to think the three of them could outwit... damn it all, she was going to jump.

"Yaaaarrrrrggggghhhh," she cried and leapt over the edge. For a moment she felt she was flying, if she spread her arms she'd soar away. It was like when she was dancing, floating, twirling, balancing…

Her right foot struck the saddle, arms spread to give her balance. The foot slid over the saddle and her body slammed down on top of it. Her weight took her on, she was starting to fall. She flung out her left arm and hooked it around the pony's neck.

Nikolai still held the reins and she could hear him urging the ponies on. A weight fell on top of her, startling her and the pony. It was the guard – he'd jumped too. The pony reared up, the guard's arm wrapped around her waist. He was too heavy, the momentum of his jump was taking him off Kat's pony – and his arm was about to wrench her with him.

The pony returned its front feet to the ground. As it did so Kat slung her right arm around its neck as well and allowed herself to roll off the pony's back while still keeping her left leg curled over the saddle – she was riding the pony on its side. The man's arm slid off her and he was gone.

Kat felt the muscles in her arms and left leg sing in protest, but she clung on. Her legs were strong from dancing, and her balance was perfect. She twisted her body and slithered back into the saddle.

Nikolai was alongside her, still holding the reins as they tore along the canal. "You all right?"

Kat nodded and glanced back. The guard scrambled unsteadily to his feet, already some way off. He took out his dagger and waved it after them.

"Halt, *vor* – in the name of the Tzar, halt thief."

"*Paka*, you lumpen," yelled Nikolai. "Goodbye for ever."

She looked round at him and her laugh came back. He handed her the reins, and he laughed too as they galloped off in search of Alexei, the sack of bread bouncing happily on Nikolai's saddle.

23

K at shivered in the chill of the early morning. The sun was yawning behind the mountains. She wished they still had the furs, a couple of them would make all the difference sleeping in the open. In the night they huddled together, Alexei cupping his long arms around Kat and Nikolai to try and keep them warm.

She looked down on them as they slept on, Nikolai still cradled in Alexei's arms. "You're just a big softy, Alex," she said quietly. "That's why you need me and Nikolai to look after you – you look after us and we look after you."

"Huh," she grunted. That was it. They were like a Russian doll, the three of them – you could place one inside the other. They fitted perfectly together.

Nikolai could have ridden off and left her in the camp, at the mercy of the guard.

He didn't – he waited. And she'd watched him when they'd found Alexei, saw the smile on his face as he watched Alexei wolf down mouthful after mouthful. He was pleased to have made Alexei happy.

"Bessst potatoesss ever," insisted Alexei through a large mouthful of the best potatoes ever, even if they were raw and difficult to chew. At least they made the terrible bread taste not quite so terrible. And it would keep them alive, another day survived, another day closer to home.

"Close but how close?" whispered Kat to herself. The mountains had grown larger and larger on the horizon. They had reached the foothills but there was no sign of Bear Mountain. The food would not last for much longer, and neither would they without shelter as the nights grew colder.

The top of the sun slid between two distant mountains. Kat stared at them. They were peculiar. Two tall, thin peaks with jagged tops, like fingers – you could see the sky through the gaps. No, not fingers, they were more like claws, thought Kat, claws raised by a snarling animal ready to attack.

She smiled again – she was smiling a great deal more since they left the Winter Palace. Johann Daniel always said she had an imagination that could see beasts fly and birds swim. It's where she went in the darkest times in the Palace, into her imagination – imaging a different life, imagining home. No, not imagining home – remembering home. Sometimes it was hard to tell the difference.

The sun rose a little higher and Kat's mouth dropped open. Was she imagining it? Bear Mountain?

She turned her head away and rubbed her eyes. She looked back. Yes, the two clawed-peaks were its giant paws and the rising sun formed its head. It did look like a bear. Well, with a bit of imagination it did.

"Alexei… Nikolai… quick, wake-up, wake-up…"

She shook Alexei's shoulder.

"Look… look…" She pointed. "Bear Mountain… Bear Mountain…"

She spun around, throwing her head back.

"That's it… Bear Mountain," she cried to the sky.

Alexei rose unsteadily to his feet and just about managed to maintain his balance as Kat threw herself on to him. She wrapped her arms as far around him as she could manage.

"We're going home… we're going home."

Nikolai unrolled the map on the ground and studied it.

"So we keep on down this valley, heading east until we see the Mountain of the Crown."

It was Nikolai who spotted the next landmark two days later, even if he needed some convincing. They had walked most of the day through woods, following a track alongside a busy stream in a bubbling hurry to get somewhere – just as they were.

Nikolai was leading the way when they emerged into open ground.

"That's it," he said and stopped so abruptly Kat walked straight into the back of him. He stumbled forward.

"Oh, maybe it isn't." Second thoughts.

"It is," said Kat, rubbing her chin where it had collided with the back of Nikolai's hard head. She could see the Crown, rising sharply above them. They were in the Urals, the valley a thin slice into the mountains. They had not seen a single sign of human life, apart from the rough track they were following.

"It could be anything," said Nikolai. "A cake with candles on it. Candle-cake mountain."

"Trust your first thought," suggested Alexei, switching the reins to his other hand – they were walking to give the horse and ponies a break. "That's what my father always said."

"Easy for a giant to say," said Nikolai. "When you're as big as a mountain it's easy to believe your first thought – not so easy from down here I can tell you."

"No," interrupted Kat, "you're right, Nikolai. And look – we climb a little and there's another valley heading south, just as Johann Daniel said there would be."

"And how can a dwarf possibly question a wizard?" grumbled Nikolai.

"He's not... oh, never mind – come on, let's get into the other valley before nightfall."

Kat skipped on down the path and Alexei plodded after her, coaxing the horses on with a gentle cluck of his tongue. Nikolai sighed.

"Yeah, he's not a wizard because a normal man can send messages through a map and make fire and knock-out monks with a magic cloud. A magic map..."

Nikolai interrupted his own mumblings and cocked his head to one side. "The map..."

He hurried after the horses and pulled the rolled

map from where it was folded over the front of his saddle. He spread it across a large flat rock – a boulder that long ago broke free of the mountain and tumbled down to provide the perfect map table – and traced his finger to the end of the valley.

"Yegoshikha," he said, stopping his finger over their destination. He bent closer, searching for a clue, one to follow the eagle and the dome. Kat had shown him the skull and cross bones. Johann Daniel would have given them something. But there was nothing, just the name **Yegoshikha** and a thick black **X** to mark its spot.

"Come on Nikolai, get a move on."

Nikolai sighed again, rolled up the map and bustled after his friends.

Nothing but an X… it didn't seem very like Johann Daniel. It didn't make sense to Nikolai. Maybe Johann Daniel got bored drawing the map by the time he reached the Urals – it was a huge country after all. Would a wizard get bored?

Maybe it was all in the letter he'd written for Kat. He glanced up at Kat. Ever since they'd seen Bear Mountain she'd floated down the valley, leaping from stone to stone, singing and humming to herself (she may be a great dancer but, Nikolai decided, she was no great shakes as a singer). She insisted Johann Daniel was no wizard. Yet she too thought there was something special about the map. That it was guiding them. And still she said he wasn't a wizard. It didn't make sense.

Then again if you are a wizard would you admit to being a wizard or keep your wizardry a secret? And then swear your apprentice to keep the wizard secret as well? Nikolai shook his head. He was confusing himself.

The thing is, whether Johann Daniel was a wizard or not, marking Yegoshikha, the destination they'd risked their lives to get to, with nothing more than an X didn't seem right. He thought he'd better mention it to Kat when they set-up camp that evening.

He never did. A mountain lion saw to that. Or that's what Nikolai thought it was. They had crossed beneath Crown Mountain into the valley heading south and were following the track through some trees when they heard it, a snarled threat from the rocks above the path.

It gave them a fright and caused the horse and ponies to bolt, tearing the reins from Alexei, whose grip was loosened by his own surprise at the sudden sound.

Their shouts and the scattering of the horse and ponies scared whatever it was away – they never saw it. Might even have been a bear, suggested Alexei that evening while they huddled in the shelter of some rocks, casting nervous glances into the darkness and hoping whatever it was wouldn't have a change of heart and fancy wolfing down a child for a midnight feast. Could have been a wolf, suggested Kat.

They'd lost Kat's pony. They found the other two grazing among the trees. But of Kat's there was no sign. Perhaps the beast took it, perhaps it just kept running.

All of which pushed Nikolai's questions over the map right out of his mind.

24

"That's not it."

Kat folded her arms and stood stock still. The boys were either side of her as if positioning themselves to grab her and march down to Yegoshikha.

"That's not it – we've gone wrong somewhere."

A small town sulked below them, a blot on a landscape it was destroying. The valley down which the Yegoshikha River ran was nothing like its neighbours. There was a sweetness in those Ural valleys, if you can imagine that. Kat knew she wasn't imagining it because she asked the boys.

"The air tastes good doesn't it – and the water, it really is sweet to drink, isn't it?" The boys nodded. "I must have tasted it before, when I was little – I remember the streams, I do… I'm sure I do."

Over the previous day Kat's excitement had grown with every step towards Yegoshikha until it crackled about her. It was catching. Alexei's usual deadpan face took a holiday. He strode along beaming and whistling. Nikolai chattered away, not really being listened to by the others and not really caring either – he just wanted to get his happy thoughts out into the world.

It was the smell that first began to change their mood. They were climbing the side of the neighbouring valley, following a narrow path upwards. Alexei caught it first.

"What's that?"

They stopped and all three sniffed the air like startled rabbits sensing danger. There was a faint whiff of rotten eggs.

"Urrrggghh," said Nikolai.

Kat said nothing, just narrowed her eyes and quickened her step.

The smell grew as the track steepened. They reached the top and looked down.

"That's not it," repeated Kat for a third time.

"It must be," said Nikolai.

"No," insisted Kat. "I do not come from..." she

raised a hand and pointed at the town cluttering up the valley floor… "THERE."

Smoke belched from the tallest of the seven large chimneys that dotted the middle of the town. That's what first caught the eye. As for the rest, there was plenty else to stare at in disbelief; in particular the river, the Yegoshikha itself. It changed colour.

The river approached the town which stole its name in a confident surge of churning green water. By the time it left, the town had taken the river's soul as well. It was difficult to tell if the grey sludge that covered the surface was even moving. Around it, the lower valley slopes had been stripped of trees to feed the furnaces of the copper works. The works sat in the middle of the town, looking like it had shoved houses aside to make room for itself.

Kat sniffed, whether because of the smell or because she was close to tears Nikolai wasn't sure. It could have been both.

"That's NOT it," said Kat and stamped her foot.

"Well, where is it then?" asked Nikolai.

Kat swivelled and swung a fist in his direction. He'd been expecting a reaction since they'd stepped onto the ridge so he was ready and ducked underneath (ducking a punch was a crucial skill for a dwarf in the Court of Peter the Great).

Alexei stretched out a hand and Kat's fist disappeared inside it. She sobbed. Nikolai spat – he couldn't think of anything else to do.

"Should've stayed in Petersburg," said Nikolai and spat again, this time with feeling.

Kat rounded on him. "Yeah, and then we'd have nothing to worry about because we'd be DEAD."

Alexei placed a hand on both their heads and twisted them gently to look at him. He spoke slowly, deliberately, each word as if carved from stone.

"There are only three of us... against..." and here he took his hand off Nikolai's head (he felt the need to keep hold of Kat) and swept it around them... "against all this. If it's not all three of us, then none of us will survive. We'll all be dead, wherever we are."

He took his hand off Kat's head and sat down, drained by the one of the longest speeches of his life.

"Now," he said, "open Johann Daniel's letter and then we'll go down and find your mother and father."

Kat put her hand to her mouth and then slipped it under her armpit. She still had the pouch tied there.

"Oh, the letter…" she said.

"Open it when you reach Yegoshikha… it's what he said."

"You open it, Alexei," said Kat, pulling it out of the pouch and offering it to him. All of a sudden she was nervous about reading it.

Alexei shook his head.

"Why not? Please…"

"Can't read."

"Nikolai?"

He sat down on Alexei's other side, disappearing from sight.

"It's your letter – you read it." His voice squeezed round Alexei's bulk.

Kat sighed and looked at the folded piece of paper, sealed with a large, red blob of candle wax. Johann Daniel had pressed his ring into the wax while it was still hot, imprinting his crest, an open book with a crown on its pages. Tzar Peter had it created for him.

She slid her thumbnail beneath one corner. When they reached Yegoshikha. She glanced down at the town. It seemed to glower up at her: *Think you're too good for your home town now, do you missie, with your Palace airs and la-di-dah graces?*

A bell, deep and insistent, sounded in the town and a memory flickered to the front of her mind. It was the factory bell. But it wasn't the bell she remembered. It was what it signalled – 'time to go home'. Men, dark, faceless shapes from this distance, emerged from the bleak factory. This was her memory; her Papa coming back from work. She didn't like it when he came home. He shouted at her Mama and swung his belt at her and then at Kat if she hadn't finished whatever it was she was supposed to have finished. It hurt, she remembered that.

This was Yegoshikha, her Yegoshikha, the town she'd been taken from. She shook her head, denying her own memory.

"No," she said.

"Open the letter, Katinka," said Alexei, patting the ground beside him. "Open it and read it to us, little sister."

Kat sat down and snuggled into Alexei. He put an arm around her and squeezed her shoulder. She broke the seal and unfolded the paper.

"My dearest Katinka Dashkova… I cannot help but smile when I write your name for it is my favourite name in all Russia. I shall write it one more time, as I hope to see you one more time. Katinka Dashkova.

"Of course that is little more than wishful thinking by a fragile man, although if you are reading this looking down on Yegoshikha…"

"See," interrupted Nikolai, "a wizard – he knows and he'll save us. I knew it."

"Shhh," said Alexei.

"…looking down on Yegoshikha then the three of you have done well. If you can cross the Steppe unharmed then you are born to survive and, I dearly hope, thrive in your new life."

Kat paused and looked up. She felt a lump in her throat and a twist in her stomach. She didn't want to read on because she knew he would not be writing with good news.

"Survive and thrive? Huh, fat chance," said Nikolai's voice. He was still hidden by Alexei.

Kat glanced down again at the letter. His handwriting was small and neat. This time she read to herself.

"*I write to inform you about your family, your birth family. I did not tell you this when you were planning your escape from the Winter Palace because I did not* want you to abandon your journey. If you stayed here I would be writing to you in the grave. You had to go.

"You come from Yegoshikha, the Yegoshikha you are looking down on. This is where you lived until you were six-years-old. I hear the town has changed but I fear the Home you believe you were born in exists only in your head. It is made from your distant memories of trips into the wild valleys surrounding Yegoshikha and stories you read in books here in the Tzar's great library. You imagined a happy childhood amid the cruelties of the Palace.

"When you first arrived I read to you but you learnt quickly – far quicker than the Tzar's daughters. The first book you read, and your favourite, was a collection of short poems and drawings of village scenes from around this great country. There was one of a hunter returning to his home village ahead of winter. You would stare at it for an age. It was called the Homecoming and now you are on a Homecoming.

"I do not know your father, Ivan, or your mother, Irina, and I do not judge them. It is, I am led to believe, a hard life in Yegoshikha. Most now work in the copper factory, a ghastly place. But life before was hard too. It has always been a poor place. That I suppose is the reason they did what they did. I dearly hope they thought you would have a better life in the Winter Palace than you could ever have with them.

"Forgive my supposing, only I want to believe the best of them. So what did they do? My dear Katinka, the X alongside their names you discovered in the Tzar's records is significant. For it means, my dear, your parents took money to hand you over to an agent of the Tzar, a man who would cross the country looking for children and animals to take for the Kunstkamera.

"The agent arrived in a town and instructed anyone who might be of interest to His Imperial Highness to assemble outside the governor's house. Your parents would have brought you and the agent must have liked what he saw for he paid coin for you. You would have been taken the following day from your home on Kama Street.

"Whatever you decide to do now, and I understand how hard this discovery will be on you, you must not come back here. You must be brave and find a life for yourselves somewhere out there. Be yourselves, my dear Katinka, be strong.

"I am not strong, I never stood up to the Tzar or his friends despite the cruelty I saw every day to you and *many, many others. And I did not have the courage to ruin your dreams with the truth before you left. Forgive me.*

"I doubt your parents are strong either – try not to judge me or them too harshly. Perhaps you should give them a second chance. Does not everyone deserve a second chance? Go and find them Katinka, you are their daughter, their flesh and blood, and they will love you."

Kat let the paper fall from her hands. It floated to the ground.

"What does it say?"

She didn't answer Alexei. Instead she stood up and walked away from them. She stared at her town. Somewhere down there were her parents, the parents who sold her to the Tzar. She wondered whether they ever thought of her.

She turned back to the others. Nikolai held the letter in his hand, he whispered to Alexei then looked up at her.

"Kat…" he began.

"I want to be wanted." She shrugged. "That's all. Wanted for me, every bit of me. I am what I am."

A thick tear rolled down her cheek. She let it fall but sniffed to try and stop others following.

"So do I." Alexei spoke softly. "I am what I am."

Nikolai looked from Kat to Alexei and back again. He folded the letter and slid it into his pocket.

"I am what I am," he said and spat on the ground.

Alexei stood up. "We should go down and find your parents. We don't know what happened. Perhaps they were made to sell you, perhaps it's a mistake, perhaps Johann Daniel made a mistake…"

"Wizards don't make mistakes," asserted Nikolai.

Kat shook her head. She felt tired.

"Nikolai…" she began.

"He is Kat, he is, you just won't admit it."

25

When a giant, a dwarf and a girl with a crooked back walk down the street together it will cause a stir. People stare. Some cross the road.

There was no chance of Kat, Alexei and Nikolai slipping through Yegoshikha unnoticed. They left the horse and the remaining pony among the trees up on the ridge, thinking that would make them less conspicuous, but a group of boys loitering on a street corner spotted them as they entered town. The boys laughed and one even threw a stone. It fell short of his target – Nikolai. The bully always aims for the smallest.

Alexei turned around and took a giant step towards them. He raised his fists menacingly and growled. The boys turned and ran.

The rest of town was quiet. They hurried along, looking for Kama Street.

"There," said Nikolai, who had the map rolled up and draped over one shoulder – it was far too precious to leave with the horses. Kama Street faced a bend in the river and had houses on one side. They were little better than log huts, small and dark, with a single little square window. Smoke trickled out of each chimney, curling up to join the thicker puffs coming from the factory that towered above the far end of the street.

Opposite the houses was a curved straggle of drooping trees. Through the trees and across a stretch of rough ground they could see the river, which here marked the town boundary. Beyond it wooded slopes rose quickly into the mountains. The river was still its proper colour – the change came after the factory – and its dark green waters provided the only break in the greyness draped across everything else.

"There…" said Kat and stopped. She pointed across the road to one of the houses. It was no different to the one on its right nor the one on its left. "This one."

"Are you sure?" Alexei studied it.

"I'm sure."

"What shall we do?" Nikolai touched the map, as if for reassurance. It had got them this far, it would take them where they needed to go.

Kat didn't reply. Instead she crossed the road and knocked on the door. Nikolai made to follow but Alexei put a hand on his shoulder.

"She must do this alone."

Kat felt her heart pumping as she knocked on the door. She had no idea what she was going to say. "Hello mother, it's the daughter you sold like a basket of eggs." "Hello mother, I'm home." "Hello mother, why?"

The door opened.

A round-faced, red-cheeked woman stood there, a broom clutched in one hand. She wore a grey smock with an apron tied to her front. Her hair was hidden beneath a faded blue scarf.

"What?" Her voice was as expressionless as her face.

Kat faced her mother. She opened her mouth, and closed it again because no words would come out.

"What?"

"M… m… m…" Kat tried to force the word from

her mouth but it would not budge. Her mouth felt dry.

"Cat got your tongue, girl?"

The woman looked up and down the street. Her eye caught sight of Alexei and Nikolai. They had retreated to the trees and were sitting beneath one.

"What's going on? Who are they?"

She looked back down at Kat and at last there was something identifiable in her face. Suspicion.

"What d'you want? Who are you? Go away…"

She started to shut the door. Kat held up a hand.

"M… m… mother…" she said.

The door closed with a bang. Kat stepped back, her head dropped. Across the road Alexei and Nikolai stood up. The door opened again. Kat looked up.

"Katinka?"

"Mother?"

The woman looked up and down the street again. "In here, quick."

She pulled Kat into the house and shut the door. It was gloomy inside. Kat blinked. There was a familiarity to the room, the stove at the far end with the shelf above it – that was where they, her mother and father, slept, the warmest place in the house.

The rough wooden table and bench, the seat by the window, the uneven floor with its thin covering of dirty straw. Each glance shoved a memory to the front of her mind. Her head pounded.

The woman, her Mama, stood a few feet away, arms folded, broom still held tight. The dim light made it impossible to be certain of the look on her face.

"Why have you come back? Are you in trouble? You don't belong here anymore."

A thick silence fell over the room. They stared at each other. Kat wondered why she felt empty. She wondered if this woman, her Mama, felt empty too. That's what it seemed like.

A pot bubbled on the stove.

"Tsk," said the woman. She hurried over to the stove, lent the broom against the wall, picked up a cloth and grasped the handle of the pot.

"Would you like some? It's not much, my porridge, but it's warm."

She reached up and took a bowl from the shelf, spooned steaming porridge into it and banged it on the table. She took two spoons and laid them either side of the bowl. She pulled out the bench and sat down. She stirred the porridge and blew on it then took a careful mouthful, muttered something and blew on it again. All without casting a single glance at Kat.

"Do you remember your mama's porridge? Used to be your favourite thing. 'Mama powig, mama powig,' you'd say, sit at the table and wave your spoon. Huh…"

She took a mouthful, head bent low over the bowl. She swallowed it and pushed the other spoon along the table towards Kat.

"Mama… I…" she began. But she could think of nothing to say.

"It wasn't my choice."

"What?"

"He decided. It was him. I didn't… well, I mean… it was him."

"Papa?"

"Papa – huh, he's no papa."

"How much?"

"Eh? What?"

"How much was I worth to you?"

"It wasn't like that Katinka, nothing like that. It was him, all him, not me… we couldn't keep you, you see. Because you were, you were… well, you were…"

227

"A freak. Touched by magic. Don't worry I've heard every description under the sun of what I am, mother…"

Kat spat the last word out. She felt her heart go cold.

The clang of the town bell made Kat jump.

"He'll be back soon, wanting his dinner. He won't be pleased to see you. He'll find out why you're here, he'll get it out of you."

"Why I'm here… why do you think I'm here?"

The woman shrugged. "You want money? We have no money – what you see is what we've got. He drank most of it away – sold you and drank your money away, that's my dearest Ivan Dashkov."

She picked up the bowl and carried it back to the stove. She stood over the stove and her shoulders shook. A strange sound came from her, a low wail. She turned and faced Kat, her face crumpled, like all the bones had been removed leaving a twisted mess of eyes, mouth and nose.

"My Katinka… my Katinka…"

Kat said nothing.

The woman, her Mama, raised her hands towards Kat, they shook.

"He'll be here any moment, you must go, you must go… he'll… he'll…"

"Sell me into slavery – shout at me – hit me… what could he do to me that he's not already done."

The door opened and she spun round.

The man shut the door quickly behind him. His face was in darkness. He was not a big man nor a small man.

"Thought I might find her here."

His voice was flat, monotone. He stepped forward. Kat could not recognise a single thing about him. She'd expected that when she saw her father's face memories would flood back.

But they didn't. Nothing stirred her mind. There was nothing remarkable about his face, nothing to recall. Nothing remarkable about his clothing, his hair (was it brown? Mousy perhaps?), or the make-up of his body, or his clothes – they were as grey as his face.

He was the faceless man. But he was her father, her flesh and blood. Part of her make-up was his. Was she faceless? She'd never thought so when she looked in one of the Princess' mirrors in the Palace. She liked her face.

He walked over to the table and slid onto the

bench. He sat with his back to her and began to hurriedly scoop up the porridge Kat's mother placed in front of him. He ate like he was afraid someone was going to take it from him.

Kat stood there, looking from his back to her mother's back. Neither of them wanted to look at her.

"The guard are here you know." He spoke suddenly.

"The guard?"

"Yes, two of them – all the way from St Petersburg, sent by the Tzarina herself. First news we had the Tzar was gone, God rest his soul."

"Why are the guard here?"

He stood up and stepped over the bench. He still wouldn't look at her. He glanced at the door.

"For you."

"Me?"

"Yeah, you and those two freaks over the road – saw them skulking in the trees."

"I don't… I don't understand…"

"Yeah, well, you wouldn't would you – look at you, what would a girl know, a girl like you, with that… that thing on you."

For the first time some feeling touched his voice and whispered across his face.

"They're to make an example of you three runaways. What did the guard call you? The Tzar's curious runaways, something like that…"

"Curiosities – we're part of the Curiosities, the Tzar's Curiosities."

"Are you now… well he, I mean she, the Tzarina, wants you back. She can't have you running off – you belong to her and if she lets three child freaks run off what will that say about her? A woman on the throne of Russia who can't even control the freaks."

Kat stared at him.

"They're waiting at the factory. You'll go with them – wait here, I'll fetch them."

"You will not." Kat spoke quietly. There was steel in her voice. It made her father pause. A fleeting thought bothered him.

"Eh?"

She stepped in front of the door.

"Out of my way, girl."

Kat stood there. She clenched her fists.

"Mama, Papa… if the guards take us back we'll be condemned to death. That's the punishment for runaways. The Tzarina, she hates us, people like us, me, Alexei and Nikolai – we're not people to her, we're just… just… animals. They'll kill us."

Her father shook his head. Her mother remained at the stove, her back to Kat.

"If we don't report you they'll kill us," said her father. "Now step aside at once."

"Come with us," said Kat. She stepped forward and raised her hands. "Come with us, into the mountains, we'll make a new life there, start again. Be a family…"

Her mother turned around.

"Oh, Katinka…"

Her father leapt for the door, pushing Kat aside with one arm and turning the handle with the other. He caught Kat in the face and she stumbled back against the wall. He got both hands on the handle and wrenched the door open. But instead of disappearing out the door, and off down the street to fetch the guards, he came flying back in and landed in a heap in front of Kat.

"Oooofffft-arrggh," he yelped, with more feeling than anything he'd said to Kat.

Alexei followed him in, sucking in all the light as he ducked through the doorway.

"Quick, quick." Nikolai hurried the young giant

in and shut the door behind them. "Don't think anyone saw us. Alexei thought we'd better come and keep an eye on you when we saw your father come in."

"Don't need keeping an eye on," snapped Kat and at once regretted it. "Thank you," she offered instead.

Her father used the wall to push himself upright. He eyed the two boys warily. Her mother hurried to his side to help him to his feet. He brushed her off.

"Get out of my way," he said, standing as tall as he could. Which still left him some way short of being eye-to-eye with Alexei. "If you do not stand aside you are in defiance of the Tzarina herself."

"Pah," snorted Nikolai, "stuff and nonsense."

"Papa..." began Kat. "Don't do this... Mama?"

She looked at her mother. Her mother still wouldn't look at her.

"Shall I knock him out?" wondered Alexei.

"Best to," said Nikolai.

"Nooo," interrupted Kat. "He's my father."

"So how else are we going to get away without him bringing the guard down on us? Hit him, Alexei..."

Kat's father raised his hands to stave off any blow.

"No," said Kat and this time she stamped her foot.

"We will walk out of here and leave them untouched. You will not hit my father Alexei – promise me…"

Alexei nodded. Nikolai tutted. "You're making a mistake – look at him, you can't trust him. Believe me – I've seen enough of his sort; the Palace shadows are full of them."

"No," repeated Kat. "He's my father."

"I'm not your father."

Kat ignored him. It was clear to her he didn't want to be her father, but he was and she would give him a second chance. She turned to her mother.

"Mama… let us go, give us an hour and then let him go for the guard. That'll give us a chance and stop you getting in trouble. This is the last thing I'll ever ask of you, Mama, of both of you… if I mean anything to you, please… please do this for me…"

"Shall I tie them up? Gag them?"

"No, Nikolai – we'll do nothing to them – they are *my* mother and father."

Her father stared at her. She tried to see something in his eyes, anything. There was nothing there. Perhaps it would come after she left. She turned to her mother.

"Goodbye, Mama."

Her mother stayed where she was, and said nothing.

Nikolai stepped forward. There was anger on his face – that was plain to see.

"If you betray us… if you betray your own daughter, then I'll… I'll…"

"Nikolai – come." Kat stepped outside without looking back. It was better that way, better not to look back. She'd realised that in those handful of minutes with her parents.

Alexei pulled the door tightly shut behind them.

"Where now?" he said.

Kat looked up and down the street. It was deserted.

"Back to the horses, put some distance between us and this place." Nikolai's face was still flushed with anger. "This place is evil."

They crossed the road and began walking back the way they'd come.

"STOP THEM!"

Kat's blood ran cold.

"STOP THEM!"

Nikolai whirled around. Kat's father was on the street. He was pointing at them. Her mother was framed in the doorway behind him, one hand over her mouth.

"I'm going to kill him…" began Nikolai. Before he could take a step, Alexei plunged down a huge hand to stop him.

"No," he said. "Kat – where?"

Kat spun around. "Think, think, think…" she muttered to herself.

"CALL THE GUARD…"

Ivan Dashkov stayed a safe distance from them and kept shouting. Doors up and down the street opened and men spilled out.

"The river… yes, the river…"

More memories stirred. The river: watching men cross in the half-hearted darkness of a high summer night, coming back from the mountains, a day herding or hunting or smuggling, a time before the factory and its smell and smoke possessed Yegoshikha. Watching them cross from a window. A real memory, not a slice of life borrowed from a storybook.

She glanced back at the house. Her mother still stood with a hand over her mouth, as though stopping herself from joining her husband in yelling for the guard to take her daughter away. There was the window. Kat swung her gaze to the river. There was the stump, the marker.

"Yes, the river," she said, this time louder and more confidently.

"DIMITRI – DON'T LET THEM GET AWAY – I'LL GO FOR THE GUARD."

"This way," said Kat and ran through the trees for the river. The bridge, the underwater bridge – if it was still there they might get away.

It was an idea as old as the hills that rose around Yegoshikha, hills full of secrets and hides. Life here had always been dangerous. Tribes came and went, enemies changed, bandits and Cossacks replacing the old foes from the east. But they still needed fighting – or fleeing from.

And what better escape route than an underwater bridge, a row of slippery planks fixed together just beneath the surface, invisible to the outsider. In quieter times, in the pauses between the fighting, they were a smuggler's delight. A way to come and go less noticed.

An underwater bridge was much easier to build than a proper bridge, even if it did need repairing every spring. But they were trickier to use. For a start they were underwater, often in a poor state, the planks happy to tip you into the water and the water itself flowing swiftly around your knees, thighs or even as high as your waist. They were not for the timid – they were for the hills men who knew every step of the way. Or the desperate.

26

"STOP THEM!"

More people had come onto the street, attracted by the cries of Kat's father. A small crowd gathered, inquisitive children at the front, more cautious adults behind. This was no place to stand out from the crowd.

"IN THE NAME OF THE TZARINA – HALT."

"Wish he'd stop yelling – think we've got the idea," muttered Nikolai, and before Alexei or Kat could second guess him he'd spun round to face the crowd, who were still the other side of the trees. He ran to the treeline and raised his hands to circle his mouth.

"IN THE NAME OF KATINKA SHUT UP – JUST SHUT UP, YOU STUPID MAN – YOU TRAITOR, YOU BETRAYED YOUR OWN DAUGHTER –

YOU DESERVE TO ROT IN HELL... WHICH IS WHAT THIS PLACE LOOKS LIKE ANYWAY... SO THERE."

A surprised silence fell over the street. The only sound the rumble of furious water down the river, a drum roll of anticipation.

Kat stood on the bank. She didn't seem to have registered Nikolai's outburst. She stared at the swiftly moving water. She could make out the first few boards beneath the surface. "It's there," she said. "Look..."

"What if it doesn't go all the way across – we'll drown," said Alexei, gesturing at Nikolai to get back to them.

"The rope, see?"

Kat pointed. A rope stretched into the river, disappeared out of sight but then re-emerged defiantly to meet the far bank.

"Think we'd better go." Nikolai was back. He'd run from the trees.

"Eh?" Kat turned round. A grumble grew from across the street. Far from shutting them up, Nikolai's outburst had the opposite effect. Urged on by Kat's father, the men began crossing the road. One carried a spade which he brandished like a club, others held broomsticks. Another had a sword with a rusty, curved blade.

"SEIZE THEM!" Kat's father was in full voice again.

"Here…" Alexei pulled his shirt over his head. "Tie this around you both and the rope – it should stop you getting washed away."

"What about you?"

"Don't worry about me – I'll follow." He knotted one arm of the shirt around each of their waists. "Go on – go, don't look back till you've made it."

Kat stepped onto the first plank, slipped and fell. She scrabbled for the rope, feeling the water trying to pull her downstream. These bridges were for summer use – by autumn the flow of the river, filled to the brim with rainwater, was becoming too strong. It washed over her head but only for a moment then she had the rope. She spat water out. It had a funny taste.

"We're too light – it needs a man's weight." A man's weight would push the planks down and allow them to walk/drag themselves across clinging to the rope.

"Alexei – you go first."

"They'll catch us… I must stop them…"

"They won't follow – they're too scared… come on."

Alexei scooped up a large stone from the river bank. With a grunt he heaved it in the direction of the mob. The stone thudded into the ground in front of them but did its job. For the moment no-one was prepared to take another step.

Alexei waded into the water and the planks sunk beneath his heavy tread. He put one hand on the rope, reaching the other back to seek a hold on Kat and the shirt that connected her to Nikolai.

"Wait," said Nikolai. He was standing on the edge of the bank, the shirt sleeve tugging at his waist. "The map." He loosened it from his shoulder and held it above his head. "Take it."

Alexei was going to refuse – what did a map matter? – when he caught the look on Nikolai's face. He wrapped it around his neck like a scarf, sucked all the air he could into his lungs and set off.

They stepped out onto the bridge and the waters roared, drowning all other sound.

If you ever find yourself in a situation where life is hanging by a thread, or the threads of a shirt sleeve to be precise, it is impossible to have a real idea of how long something takes. Time plays tricks.

Minutes become hours, seconds an eternity. To Kat it seemed to take forever to cross the Yegoshikha River but it could only have taken a handful of minutes because they were always moving and it wasn't a wide stretch of water.

They made it thanks to Alexei's strength and Kat and Nikolai's ability to cling on for dear life, and life had never felt so dear to Kat as she swallowed and spat out mouthful after mouthful of odd-tasting water. The second time she went under she lost her red ballet shoes, plucked from her pocket by the current and whisked away, a flash of red then they were gone.

Anger flooded through her and carried her across. She wanted to live and nothing was going to stop her, not this silly river, not her horrible father, nor a mother who didn't seem to care about her own daughter, nor mad monks, cruel Boyars, Princes, Dukes or anyone else with a dumb title, nor any of the Preobrazhensky Guard in their silly green and red uniforms. None of them. Damn Them.

The taste of the river remained in her mouth as

she lay on the far bank, gasping for breath. Nikolai lay beside her. She could hear his ragged breathing.

Alexei was wringing out his shirt, his great hands squeezing out the water. He was also keeping an eye on the far bank. The mob collected around the start of the underwater bridge but nobody was prepared to make the crossing, both through fear of the bridge itself and the knowledge that first across would be confronted by Alexei.

He could see Kat's father pointing at the men then at the bridge, demanding they cross. There was plenty of head shaking and pointing, lots of sayers but no doers. Not like us, thought Alexei.

He wrung one last squeeze out of his shirt and pulled it over his head. It clung to him.

Across the river two men in uniform, a familiar uniform, were pushing their way through the mob. The first to the bank raised a red-sleeved arm and pointed across the river. The other joined him and with his red-sleeved right arm drew his sword. He prodded at the nearest man. The man shook his head so the red-sleeve lifted the sword higher and pressed the point against the man's throat. The man nodded this time – carefully so his skin remained in one piece – and when the guard lowered his sword the man stepped ever so gingerly on to the first plank of the underwater bridge. He took two steps, lost his footing and in a flash was swept away downstream his arms waving a desperate farewell; the red-sleeve lifted the sword again and another man was prodded forward.

"We must go," said Alexei, putting out a hand for Kat. "Here…"

She took it, then put hers out for Nikolai. He picked up the map – it was a little damp and a couple of the drawings were smudged but otherwise it had survived the crossing undamaged.

"Where?" wondered Nikolai.

"This way," instructed Kat and led them into the trees.

Their feet squelched as they ran. Kat's were slipping in her sodden boots, rubbing her skin. If her feet became blistered or too raw to stand on they were finished. She took her boots off and slung them over her shoulder. The bare ground, sprinkled with pine needles, felt cool beneath her feet. Alexei and Nikolai copied her.

They climbed in silence, wet clothes sticking to

them, following a path winding upwards through the trees. The woods were quiet, as if listening to the sounds drifting up from the river. Shouts reached them – one by one more of the mob and the Guards were getting across. Once they had numbers they would start the hunt.

"Kat – do you know where we're going?" Nikolai was always the questioning one.

"I… I think so…"

"You think so? Excuse me…" He stopped to take a deep breath – the path was getting steeper. "We've a mob chasing us and you 'think' you know where you're going…"

"Leave her be," said Alexei. He was in the rear, finding the going harder as he discovered a fact of giant life: giants go downhill much better than up.

"I've been here before… I remember…"

"Your memory Katinka has already got us…"

Kat, who was leading, rounded on Nikolai. Hands on hips she looked furiously down on him. She wanted to shove him, shove him in the chest and send him tumbling down the hill. She could feel the anger pulsing through her. So could Nikolai. She raised her hands, she wanted to do this, really wanted to. And

Nikolai could see that too. He flinched and that was enough.

"Oh, Nikolai... I..."

It wasn't Nikolai she should be angry with, she knew that, but that fire in her belly, that's what kept her going, kept her fighting. If that went out she would be finished as surely as if her feet were too sore to walk on. She picked up a stone and hurled it downhill as hard as she could. It cracked off a tree and dived into the undergrowth. Kat took a deep breath and set off again.

"I've been up here before... I know it."

She threw her words over her shoulder at Nikolai. "I know I've got us into a bit of a hole but..."

"No, I wouldn't," butted in Nikolai. "I wouldn't rather be back in the Palace, I'd rather be here with you and Alexei... although to be honest I'd prefer not being chased by a mob who want to tear us to pieces."

Kat frowned in concentration. "This path it goes high into the woods... I remember a rope bridge – we went as far as a rope bridge but he wouldn't let me over, said it was too dangerous for a wee girl..."

"Who? Your father?"

"No... not my father..."

"Your mother?"

"No."

"Who?"

"I… I'm not sure, I can't remember, not properly. I remember eyes…"

"Eyes?"

"Blue. Pale blue, like the sky on a clear day across the steppe."

"Who?"

"Dunno… I really don't know."

There was a new sound rising to meet them, the insistent bark of dogs, straining to be let off the leash.

"Run," said Alexei. He needn't have bothered – Kat and Nikolai were already tearing up the path. He took a deep breath and set off after them.

27

The noise of the dogs was growing. These were not dogs to pat and play with, to throw sticks for and tickle their tummies. These were hunting dogs, whipped up by their handlers and let go in a fury.

Kat swallowed and looked down the hill. The forest had taken a breather and they were standing in open ground, at the top of a small, sloping meadow. There was no sign of their pursuers. But it would not be long. She turned back to the gorge.

It was not wide – the length of two Alexei's perhaps – but wide enough to need a bridge, and that was the problem.

There was a bridge and it was a rope bridge, so what she remembered was correct. Only instead of going across, the bridge went down, straight down into the gorge. At the bottom a stream picked its way around savage looking rocks whose jagged edges stabbed angrily upwards.

"So…" began Nikolai. Kat shook her head.

"I told you the bridge was here – how was I to know it's broken?"

"They're close," said Alexei. He bent down and picked up two large stones.

"No," barked Nikolai. "Put them down…"

"I need something… the dogs, they'll rip us to pieces…"

"Not yet – help me." He lay down at the edge of the gorge and began trying to pull up the remains of the bridge. It was too heavy for Nikolai. But not for Alexei. Quickly he hauled up the tangle of ropes.

Nikolai ran his hands among the ropes, tugging and pulling at them.

"Here," he said. "This one… Kat untangle the rest of this one."

He took the end he'd uncovered and tied it around one of the bridge posts. He was good at knots. As a royal dwarf, knowledge of knots was a lifesaver given the number of times the Tzar demanded they swing from the ceiling, ride an elephant and once even slide down a giraffe.

Nikolai's idea came from the Winter Palace. It was the "game" he most dreaded. The one that left him black and blue. The one the nobles had last played with him moments before Kat and Alexei walked into his life.

Kat uncovered the other end of the rope and as Nikolai looped it around his shoulders and his waist before tying it in his best knot – the Tight Finn – he explained what he wanted them to do.

"No," said Alexei. "What if..."

"You're strong enough – you can get me over. The landing might hurt but I'm used to it and I know how to roll."

"It might work," suggested Kat.

"If it doesn't you'll fall to your death... those rocks..."

"Toss me – it's our only chance."

Alexei shook his head. "It's not..."

"Tis... and I'd rather die on those rocks than be an angry dog's dinner."

They were interrupted by a snarl. A black dog with a scarred muzzle was slinking towards them.

Alexei drew back his arm and flung his first stone. It slammed in front of the dog, which stopped and snarled again. White drool dribbled from its mouth. Kat could see its line of sharp teeth when it snarled. The second stone hit its target. This time the dog yelped and hurried back into the trees, tail between its legs.

"Do it – or we'll all die. Take an arm and a leg."

Alexei looked at Kat. She nodded at him.

Alexei swallowed and wrapped big hands around Nikolai's left arm and leg.

"Ready?"

It was Nikolai's turn to nod. "Hard as you can, you big clot," he said and spat on the ground.

Kat shut her eyes. So did Nikolai. Alexei picked Nikolai up, looked across the gorge, and heaved his friend as hard as he could into the air.

Nikolai opened his eyes as soon as Alexei let go, not that he could see much as he flew over the gorge. The other side approached in a blur and hurt him as he hit it hard. He landed on his side – "My head would have been better; nothing in there," he liked to joke when recounting the tale in years to come as the width of the gorge widened with each telling.

Jagging pain shot up his left arm and stabbed through his ribs. He curled himself into a ball. It was instinctive, his reaction to protect his battered body from the accompanying beating from the Tzar's courtiers.

"NIKOLAI!"

He shook his head. He wasn't curled up in Court. He was standing up for himself, and his friends. He leapt to his feet and squealed as he did so. He pressed a careful hand against his ribs and gasped.

"NIKOLAI?"

"I'm all right." Nikolai looked around, his hands now busy untying the rope. He picked a stout tree near the edge, looped the rope around his body once more then tied it to the tree. Between him, his knot and the tree it should be enough. He didn't dare think what would happen if it wasn't.

He saw Alexei hurl another stone, a yelp a moment later suggesting a hit. The dogs, and the mob, were closing in. Nikolai's head spun. He wanted to curl into a ball again. Instead he held the rope tight.

"READY," he yelled.

Kat secured the map around her neck, tucking it into her shirt. She fears nothing, thought Nikolai as he watched her lie on the rope, wrap a leg around it and pull herself out over the gorge.

Look at Katinka Dashkova. Gravity's call swivelled her body around the rope so she was now hanging from it, legs curled over the top and hands pulling her across. She was so graceful, so strong. He held tight on the rope, trying to ignore the pain cutting through his ribs as it tightened around him.

He began to sing, the song that Kat once danced to. It sprung into his mind and, before he knew it, was out his mouth. The words floated across the gorge before being swallowed by the growing hubbub on the far side.

A moment later Kat was across. Nikolai reached to help her and groaned as his ribs reminded him of the damage he'd done to them.

"Nikolai?"

"It's nothing," he said. "Here, take the rope with me, hold tight... ALEXEI, COME ON, YOUR TURN."

They watched Alexei hurl another stone, then another. He stepped backwards towards the gorge still looking down the meadow. A dog leapt for him. He heaved a meaty fist and bashed it away. Another dog sprang into view. It caught his arm. He swung his arm and his coat and shirt tore as the dog slid off, leaving bright red marks where its teeth had bitten into his flesh.

Two more dogs appeared. He kicked out at one and both shied away. Alexei took another step back, looked behind him and saw nothing but the gorge. As his head turned one of the dogs went for him, thudding into his chest. He waved his arms above his head, wind-milling in a desperate attempt to keep his balance.

"ALEXEI…" Kat's sharp yell pierced the sky.

Alexei took another step back and this time his foot found nothing but thin air. The dog howled as it went down. For a moment it seemed Alexei might regain his balance. Kat stretched out an alarmed hand as if she could stop him following the dog over the edge. Her hand went over her mouth as the moment passed, and he fell.

Giants, as you will be well aware, have big hands and long arms. And it was Alexei's long right arm and huge right hand that allowed him to grab the rope as he toppled over the edge. His fingers (also large) coiled around it in a flash and his fall was checked. He dangled above the gorge.

It was then that another giant factor came into play. Giants are heavy. And the weight of a giant, even a young one, hanging from a worn old rope was only going to end one way. The rope snapped.

Alexei dropped but clung onto the rope as it swung across the gorge. He hit the rock face with enough force to drive the air from his body. Strong as an ox, he hung on.

Above him the tree the rope was tied to creaked and strained. And held. But there was another problem because the rope was still looped around Nikolai. Alexei's fall pulled it so tight Nikolai was pinned down, stuck fast, the rope digging into his shoulder, digging into his skin, the hard ground pressing against his damaged ribs. He cried out as the rope pulled even tighter. Alexei's weight was squeezing the breath from Nikolai.

Kat grabbed at the rope and pulled as hard as she could. It was hopeless. She crawled to the edge and peered over. Alexei was looking up.

"What do I do?" she said. "Nikolai's tangled in the rope. I can't... if you keep... he'll... he'll be crushed..."

Alexei closed his eyes. He only had one answer. He opened them again and looked down. If he fell straight he might, just might, plunge into the stream and it might, just might, be deep enough for him to survive. But it might not, and besides the chances of staying calm, keeping arms and legs together while plummeting downwards were slimmer than a stick insect.

"Oww!" The stone struck him between the shoulder blades. He twisted his neck. The two guards and their mob had arrived on the other side of the gorge.

Kat picked up a stone and chucked it in their direction but it lacked the power to damage her targets, who jeered at her.

Kat looked around. There was a boulder shaped like a large canon ball lying near the gorge's edge. She wished she could pick it up and fire it at the townspeople. A stone landed in front of her and scudded hard into her shins. It hurt, her eyes watered.

One of the guards stepped forward and raised a commanding hand. The mob fell silent.

"Bow and arrow? Gun?" he inquired loudly. There was a muttering and a mumbling behind him and a man was pushed forward.

"Who are you?"

"Kalashnikov, sir, the town hunter."

"You have a bow and arrow?"

"Yes, sir."

"Give it to me."

"Not here, sir, down at the house, sir."

"Fetch it, at once… wait…" The guard gestured along the gorge, "… before you go, is there another crossing?"

The hunter pointed up hill. "It's a long walk, but up there a light man can leap the gorge, needs a bold man to do it."

Dismissed, the hunter hurried off down the hill to fetch his bow and arrow. The guard barked orders, dispatching the other guard and six men to seek the crossing point.

"Now we wait," said the guard, sitting down on a rock. "And enjoy the show."

"Kat… Kat…"

Nikolai lifted his head. His voice was hoarse, his breathing ragged.

"Don't let Alexei die for me. The boulder, the round one… if you can get it… get it under the rope, here by me… it'll let me… let me breathe properly…"

"Then Alexei can climb up?"

"Must be quick… bow and arrow coming…"

"I know; they'll shoot us won't they." Kat lay down and leant over the edge, she whispered to Alexei. He explored the cliff face with his feet, and thanks to her directions found what he was looking for.

"Be quick," he said.

"Look at the girl, scuttling around like a crab." The guard roared with laughter at his words and the others joined in.

"Shall we stone them, sir?" It was Kat's father's voice.

"No, the Tzarina's orders are to bring at least one of them alive," replied the guard. "Someone needs to be made an example of."

"A few stones' ll stop them trying to escape, sir."

"Escape? They don't have a chance!"

Kat rolled the boulder next to the rope, just in front of Nikolai.

"Now," she hissed and Alexei let go of the rope. He waited to drop, but he didn't. The footholds he'd found were enough to keep him where he was, at least for a moment or two. He pressed his cheek against the cold rock and kept his feet squeezed into the footholds, one a small shelf, the other a zig-zagged crack in the cliff face. The fingers of his right hand were shoved into another crack giving him the slenderest of holds. His left hand found nowhere so stayed close to the rope. His legs were spread at an awkward angle; he was going to lose his balance if Kat wasn't quick.

He wanted to shout at her to hurry, but he knew it would be wasted words, so held his tongue.

Kat rolled the boulder and once it was in place slid the rope under it. All the time Alexei watched the end of the rope dance in front of his face, teasing him, tempting him to clutch hold again. Grab me and save yourself, it said. He waited, the longest few seconds of his life. Sweat spread across his brow.

"Now," hissed Kat once more, the boulder in place and Nikolai loosened from the rope's python-like grip. Alexei seized the rope and began to pull himself up.

"Sir… sir…" Kat's father's voice again.

It took Alexei a matter of moments to reach the top of the gorge. He dropped the rope and Kat pulled it from around Nikolai, who let out a relieved groan.

"Sir… stones, sir." Her father's voice was shrill, the increasing alarm upping the octaves. If their quarry got away someone would be blamed and there was no way a guard would shoulder any fault – particularly if there was a convenient scapegoat standing beside him.

Kat's father picked up a stone and threw it. The guard said nothing, lost for words at what he'd just seen.

"STONE THEM!" screeched Ivan Dashkov and heaved one across the gorge. It didn't make the children's side, falling noiselessly towards the stream far below, but it sparked the guard from his trance.

"STONE THEM!" He stood up and bawled his command, drawing his sword and waving it around his head. It was a sign of helplessness – there was nothing he could do to stop Kat, Nikolai and Alexei escaping. The guard had sat and watched himself outwitted. Fury surged across his face.

"KILL THEM!"

What was left of the mob scrambled for stones and flung them in the direction of the three children. But they were not like Alexei, not strong enough to hurl a stone of any dangerous size across the divide. The ones that hit their targets, and all three were hit at least once, made them cry out and left bruises but could do nothing to stop them.

Alexei scooped up Nikolai and threw him over his shoulder, drawing another howl of pain, and followed Kat into the trees. Soon they were out of sight of the gorge, the mob, the guard and Kat's father, swallowed by the forest.

28

"Slow down, you're hurting me."

"No," insisted Kat, "the other guard will be across the gorge soon. We must go higher."

It had started to rain. The heavy rain of a Russian autumn – winter was not far behind – and even beneath the canopy of the forest they were soaked through. The rain beat on the leaves above them. It was an insistent noise that added to Kat's desire to keep going... they are coming, they are coming, THEY are coming...

"Let me walk."

"No – too slow."

Nikolai's words came out in bursts as he bounced on Alexei's shoulder – he was slung over like a sack – punctuated by painful groans.

She patted him on the head.

"Get off," he said. "Let me walk."

"No – now shush let's get on."

They walked in silence for a time, climbing higher and higher. Kat shivered. It was getting colder and she was wet through. She didn't know where they were going, but didn't want to admit that to the others. They had to keep going, keep climbing, get away from the guard and those men. Get away from her father.

She'd glanced back as they left the gorge and caught a glimpse of his face. This time it was a face to remember. It was twisted. Not in anger. In fear. He was terrified. Terrified of what was going to happen to him if Kat and Nikolai and Alexei got away. He was trapped in a life of fear. Kat felt a flicker of pity for him. Poor man, living every day scared. That was no way to live. She would not be like her father.

"It's odd you know."

Kat looked round sharply. She wasn't used to Alexei starting a conversation. He stopped. There was no sound from Nikolai, his eyes were closed. He was either asleep or had passed out, probably somewhere in between.

"Your father… he didn't look a bit like you. I looked

at his face and your mother's... there was nothing of you there. You wouldn't know they're your mother and father..."

"What," interrupted Kat, "because they didn't have one of these?" She pointed at her back, she could feel the sodden material of her shirt and cloak stuck to it. It felt uncomfortable. "Because they looked 'normal'?"

She spat the last word out. Her mouth twisted into a sneer. She didn't mean it but she couldn't help it.

"No." Alexei stopped and turned to face her. He towered over her, one hand curled around Nikolai to keep him from falling. "No. It's not that. It's not that at all – I don't look at people like that, Katinka. You should know that."

He turned away from her and lengthened his stride up the slope. Kat watched him go. The rain found a way down the back of her neck, sneaking beneath the map that was still rolled up around her like a scarf. She rubbed her neck. The map felt oddly dry. *Does everyone look like their mother and father, a mishmash of both; a mother's nose and chin, a father's ears and eyes?*

"Alexei... Alexei..." She hurried after him. The

rain changed, softened, became slushy, colder, icy. She shivered. They had to find shelter.

It was Kat who spotted it. The hill was steepening, more rocks appearing among the trees. She noticed a gap between a huge boulder and the hill close behind it. An inkling, a flash of a thought, told her to squeeze between them and there it was, a cave, deep enough to get out of the sleet (it wasn't far off turning into snow).

Alexei shifted Nikolai into his arms, carrying him like a baby. Alexei must be exhausted, thought Kat, as she watched him edge through the gap. But on he goes, never complaining.

They laid Nikolai down on the smooth, dry floor of the cave. He groaned. His eyes were shut. Kat took off her cloak and folded it beneath his head.

"He looks bad," she said and looked up at Alexei as if expecting him to have the answer.

"Yes," he said and sat down beside Nikolai. Kat sat on the other side, leaned over and brushed the hair from Nikolai's face.

She took the map from round her neck, unrolled it and laid it on the rocky floor. It was dry, somehow. She picked it up and draped it over Nikolai.

"It's the only thing that's not wet," she explained to Alexei.

"How?" he said.

She shrugged and lay down next to Nikolai. His breath was coming in short, sharp bursts. She stared at the roof of the cave. Three children lost in a forest. This was like the start of a fairy story, she thought. Only it feels like the end. If the men found them they would die, if they stayed out here in winter, they would die.

"Sleep on a problem," Granny Garbuchka liked to say, "and some of it goes away."

Which was easy for her to say from the warmth of the Winter Palace. Kat sighed and reached an arm over Nikolai. Alexei's hand found hers and squeezed it gently.

29

Blue eyes. They were a signal to her. No words needed. His eyes, shining. Eyes so deep you couldn't look into them without feeling yourself becoming part of him. He would stand across the river and smile and even from that distance she could see into his eyes and see she would be safe with him. That he was... he was her...

Kat opened her eyes and sucked in her breath. Blue eyes. Even in the dim early morning light of the cave, she could see his blue eyes.

"Hello," she said. Home, she thought, I've come home. She shook her head, she was tired, exhausted, delirious even, dreaming perhaps.

His face was funny, not funny as in ha-ha, funny as in strange, different.

She rubbed her own eyes and when she was done the blue eyes were still there, and this time they came with a smile. A familiar smile, crooked because his top lip was not straight like most top lips.

It had a quirk in the middle, which tried to stop the smile looking like a smile. Above it the blue eyes insisted: I am smiling at you. It was a harelip, that was the word. Or the mark of the witches, that's what they said in the country. Marked at birth by a witch – a family cursed by their first born.

"Hello, Sasha," said Kat, still lying there looking up at him. He was neither big nor small, but the way he carried himself suggested confidence in who he was. He had dark hair, as dark as coal, and seemed no more than a couple of years older than her. She didn't know where the name came from. It just popped into her head and out her mouth. Sasha, a nice name, a soft name, the name of her...

"I didn't think you'd remember. It was a long time ago... Katinka."

"Sasha," she said again, testing the name on her tongue, enjoying its familiarity. "Sasha, you came. I had a dream... I wasn't sure if you'd come..."

"I'm here, my sister."

She leapt to her feet and threw her arms around him.

"Eh?"

"What?"

Alexei and Nikolai woke together and sat up together.

"Owww," added Nikolai as the pain of his sudden rising stabbed at his damaged ribs.

Alexei continued to his feet, raising his fists as he did so.

"Who is he? Is he alone? Shall I hit him?"

Sasha took a step back, forcing Kat to let go of him, and pulled back his heavy cloak to reveal a dagger stuck in his belt. He rested a hand on it. The smile remained in place and the blue eyes swung up to Alexei.

"Easy there, big fellow."

Kat stepped forward after Sasha and threw her arms around him once more. This time she lifted her legs as well and attempted to wrap them around him. It meant Sasha had to let go of his dagger and cling on to Kat.

"My brother, my brother," said Kat, her voice

singing. The cave's walls sung it back to her. My brother, my brother.

"Your brother?"

Alexei looked confused. Nikolai was looking at the map, having just noticed it had been a makeshift blanket for him.

"Come," said Sasha. "We must go. We've a long ride ahead. There are cloaks outside on the ponies, they'll keep you warm. You can eat as we go, I have bread and pears. Can the little one ride?"

"I'm no child," snapped Nikolai. He was still in pain from his ribs but a night's sleep had restored his normal settings.

"I know," said Sasha, "but I saw you injured yesterday – can you ride with the injuries? We cannot wait here. They're searching for you. The hunter will know this cave."

"You saw me? Yesterday?"

Sasha ignored Nikolai. "Quick, follow me."

He left the cave. The boys looked at Kat.

"Weird, Kat – very weird," suggested Nikolai.

"Yes," agreed Alexei.

"My brother," said Kat and followed him out of the cave.

Outside four ponies, stout mountain beasts with broad backs and strong, stubby legs, stood patiently.

"Here," said Sasha, handing her a cloak. It was cut from deer skin and lined with fur. She felt warmer the moment she put it on and pulled it tight around her, the fur tickling her neck and chin.

He gave one to Alexei and Nikolai as well. Alexei's was too small, Nikolai's too big. They were used to that.

Nikolai tried and failed to mount his pony. The pain in his ribs was too much.

"Need we tie him on?" asked Sasha. "We have no time for fooling around."

Nikolai glared at him, handed Alexei his cloak and put his foot in the stirrup. He gasped as he swung his leg over and once more as he came to rest on the pony's back.

"I'll ride first, then Kat, then the little one and last you, big fellow," said Sasha, pointing at Alexei. "We must ride in silence, unless the little one falls off…"

"Stop calling me little one."

"He's Nikolai, and he's Alexei." Kat pointed at

them each in turn. "And this is Sasha... Sasha, my brother."

The smile that followed stretched from ear to ear.

30

The snow began around an hour into the ride. It fell quickly and quietly, deadening the sounds of the forest and the mountains as it tumbled from the grey sky.

Sasha looked round, a flash of blue amid the grey and white, to check on them. They were fine. All they had to do was sit tight, hold onto the reins and ride with the roly-poly rhythm of the ponies' progress as they plodded up and up, higher and higher into the Urals.

Kat watched the snow settle on her pony's neck. She dug her heels into his sides, encouraging him to close the gap on Sasha. As the snow thickened, great white flakes spinning and sliding from the sky, twisting and turning in happiness at their first outing of winter, it was becoming harder to see her brother. She'd lost him once in her life and wasn't going to run the risk of it happening again.

She swivelled in her saddle to see if Nikolai had kept up. Behind him she could just make out the shadowy bulk of Alexei. She turned back to the front and settled into her saddle, raising her shoulders to drop her neck lower into the cloak's warming embrace.

How long was it since she'd last seen him? For once it didn't bother her, Katinka the Precisionist. Because she'd forgotten him, he'd been wiped from her conscious mind, exiled to exist only in her dreams. Now that he was here, in front of her she remembered... how he would come to her parents' hut in town. She'd look out the window and see him standing by the underwater bridge. She'd slip out and run to him. He'd take her across, surefooted, and they'd disappear into the woods, wandering around as he revealed its secrets, the berries you could eat and ones that would mean death if a drop of its juice touched your lips. He dug up roots that tasted better than Mama's porridge and the bitter ones that were tough to eat but would keep you alive. He showed her the tracks of wolves, the paw prints of bears, the scuttle of a wildcat.

All this she'd shut away, locked the memory box and thrown away the key. He'd told her he was her brother. Appeared from nowhere one day when she was playing by the river. Sat with her and said, "Hello, Katinka, I'm your brother Sasha."

And that was it. She was little. She needed no explanation. If he was her brother, why didn't he live with her and Mama and Papa? Why did Mama and Papa never talk of him? Why did he never come to see them, or take them into the woods? She never asked anything of him. She accepted him for who he said he was in the simple way little children do. This was Sasha, her brother.

After all, why would anyone pretend to be Her brother?

She thought hard, trying to ignore the cold creeping across her face, making her eyes smart. When did she forget him? And what were the answers to the questions she never asked?

In the Winter Palace they forced you to grow up before your time, snatching the wonders of childhood away. She found comfort in the library with Johann

Daniel, in his stories, in his books, his drawings and paintings.

Palace life was a daily struggle. There was no time for memories. She shut Sasha out. In his place came the pretty village in the mountains, the crystal clear waters and the house with the blue onion domes. Pictures stolen to hang inside her mind instead of her own memories.

Who are you Sasha? Who am I? She rode in a trance, looking in every corner of her mind for an answer and finding none.

They left the trees behind, picking their way round the side of a mountain, the ponies slipping and sliding on the frozen track. It took them into a pass, mountains clambering on either side to see which one could touch the sky first.

The skies cleared for a time in the afternoon. The mountains were covered in snow, everywhere Kat looked there was another peak. The path snaked on, finding an opening where the eye could see none.

They slept that night in another cave. Sasha lit a small fire in the entrance – if he'd lit it inside the smoke would have overwhelmed them as they slept – and they clustered around it sucking its warmth inside them. He'd taken the wood from a pile hidden at the back of the cave. It was not the first time he had been here.

"I know these mountains," he said when Nikolai pestered him to tell more. "I've been here all my life. I heard you were coming so I kept a look out for you, spotted you riding for Yegoshikha and followed you. I knew who you were as soon as I saw you – I mean I knew who Katinka was."

"How could you know we were coming?"

Sasha ignored Nikolai's question, instead he lay down, pulling his cloak around him. "Sleep – we've another hard day's ride ahead tomorrow. All being well we'll make Golovina before dark,"

Golovina. Kat rolled the word around her mouth, testing it. It fitted. She lay down and closed her eyes.

"What's Golovina when it's at home?" wondered Nikolai. He stared into the fire for a moment, nodded, then unrolled the map. He bent his head close, tilting the map so it caught the fire's flickering light. "I just want to check... saw something this morning..."

He gasped. "Look." He prodded a finger on the

map, crumpling a part of it. "The cave... look, eyes... blue eyes – they are aren't they? Look, Alexei."

Alexei shook his head. He wanted no part of this.

On went Nikolai's finger, pressing harder against the map's soft surface. "Here, a house, blue domes... Golovina."

He looked up and Alexei could see the surprise in his eyes. A spark spat from the fire. It landed on the map, then another and another. Nikolai swept the first away and the second and the third but by then there was a fourth and a fifth and a sixth. They kept coming and one became a flame, at first a flash of blue, of course blue.

"Whoof," said the map as it caught fire.

"Ah," said Nikolai. He tried to flap out the flames, crush them with a corner of his cloak but only fanned them. They spread.

"Ahhhh," said Nikolai. He stood up and brushed the burning map off him. It fell on to the fire and before you could count to 10 (or nine to be precise and keep Kat happy) it was gone.

Nikolai sat down. Neither Kat nor Sasha stirred.

"He burnt it," said Nikolai. He looked up at Alexei. "He burnt it."

"You did," said Alexei. "You burnt it."

"No, no, no." Nikolai's eyes were wide. "HE burnt it. The wizard – he burnt it."

"What? Johann Daniel? Burnt the map? How?" Alexei stood up and peered into the dark. "You saw him? Here? Just now?"

"No, but…"

Alexei sat down again and gathered his cloak around him. "Well then."

Nikolai sighed. "Don't you see?"

"It's dark," said Alexei. "I can see nothing beyond our circle."

"Golovina… that's where we've been coming all along – don't you see, Alexei?"

There was an urgency to his voice. He needed Alexei to see. Alexei didn't, or wouldn't.

"Everything on the map has been guiding us here."

"To this cave?"

"Nooo, don't be stupid."

"I'm going to sleep," said Alexei. "You heard what he said, we've a long ride ahead."

He lay down and pulled the cloak over his head, signalling he was done with whatever nonsense Nikolai was spouting.

"Guiding us… it has guided us," muttered Nikolai to himself. He stared into the flames, watching the last corner of the map curl up and disappear to ashes. "He's watched us every step of the way, and now we're here, safe with Sasha, he's taken it back."

Nikolai lay down and snuggled inside the cloak – being able to wrap it twice around himself meant he would be warmer than the others. There was a definite advantage of being little. His ribs ached but he could put up with the pain now he was safe. He was used to being black and blue.

"You're right, aren't you?" he asked himself as he closed his eyes. Tiredness overwhelmed him and he was asleep before he could answer his own question.

31

Kat shrugged when Nikolai told her about the map. He watched her carefully, waiting for her to erupt. The thing with Kat, Nikolai had learned, was never try and second guess her, just be ready. Her fiery temper meant she could boil at any moment.

So when she shrugged, he flinched. Because he'd failed to follow his own advice and was expecting what he expected – and Kat, as usual, did the unexpected.

The Kat of a few weeks ago, even a few days ago, would have flown into a fury at the loss of Johann Daniel's precious map.

"We don't need it anymore – we've found Golovina. You know I dreamed of Golovina last night."

She turned and walked over to where her pony was tethered, gathered the reins and slid easily into the saddle. The pony looked cross. Perhaps, considered Nikolai for a moment, the poor beast had soaked up her bad moods. Then again ponies look cross most of the time.

"You knew?" Nikolai followed her and stroked the pony's nose as he spoke. "About the map, that it was sending us here?"

"What d'you mean?"

"Magic, Kat... wizardry, that's what I mean."

She shook her head. "You don't give up do you?" She looked up the snow-covered valley. "At anything – you don't ever give up."

"Come on," said Sasha, digging his heels into his pony's flanks. "Or we'll leave you for the wolves."

"Wolves?" said Nikolai, hurrying for his pony. Alexei lifted him up – it was still painful for him to try and climb on. "There are wolves here?"

"Of course," said Sasha, his blue eyes shining in the morning sun. "This is the Urals, we have everything."

"Even wizards I warrant you," said Nikolai as he gripped his legs around his pony and urged it forward, although he said it too quietly for anyone else to hear.

It was a beautiful morning, matching their rising

spirits. Nikolai began to sing until Sasha quietened him with a hissed "Shhhhhh."

"Snow slides," he explained. "The first snows can loosen rocks, noise can set off an avalanche and we'll be crushed. Or suffocated, your mouth and nose filled so full with snow you can't breathe."

"Oh," said Nikolai. Quietly. He looked up at the mountains and wondered if anyone had ever been to the top. He felt small, not because of his body, not because he'd been born different to most people, but small because of where they were, in these gigantic mountains that made all men the size of mice.

The ponies were strong, stepping determinedly up the valley, sometimes thigh deep in snow. They struggled along a pass and then the route dropped down, quickly, the path winding its way across a hillside, beneath them a wooded valley.

On the valley floor they disappeared into the trees. The snow was thinner here and as they kept going down it grew thinner still until it was no more than a sprinkle of icing on a cake.

Kat spent most of the day in a happy haze, humming (quietly) to herself and watching Sasha's shoulders roll as he pushed his pony on through the snow. He carried the reins in one hand, resting the other on his hip. He looked like a knight of old riding out to battle.

The high spaces of the mountains, the sky so far and so blue above them, the sun sparkling on the snow, was replaced by the tightness of the forest. Trees clustered around them. The wind stirred and it sounded as though the trees were whispering.

"Who are you?"

"How dare you pass through here?"

"We're watching you… we're watching you…"

And she felt she was being watched. She sat up in her saddle and glanced around. Nikolai was asleep, Alexei's eyes were glazed over. She could see nothing but trees and bushes.

Her pony snorted. It made her heart jump. She looked around again. Someone was shadowing them. She was sure of it. She shuddered.

"Sasha… Sasha…"

A horse whinnied. A horse, not a pony. Kat swung her eyes left. There was a black horse. A bearded man wearing a thick, dark fur hat and a dark coat sat atop of it. He held a sword in his left hand, the blade resting over his shoulder. He made no move to come closer, just sat on his horse and studied them.

"Sasha… Sasha…"

Ahead the trees were thinning and she could make out a meadow, green and snowless, where the forest ended.

"Sister?"

Sasha swivelled in his saddle and Kat copied him so she could point to the man they had passed. He was gone.

"A man…" she said. "With a sword… he was there, I saw him."

"Go ahead," instructed Sasha, "ride out into the meadow. I'll catch you up."

He tugged the reins and his pony stepped aside to let the other three past.

Kat looked back. Sasha was gone. She swallowed and dug her heels in. She wanted to get into the open as quickly as possible. The pony broke into a reluctant trot and the other ponies copied without waiting instruction from their riders. The sudden increase in speed shook Nikolai awake.

"Eh, what? Where's the map?" he slurred as he was dragged from his dreams.

They were already out of the forest and into the brightness of the sunshine. Once they had some distance between themselves and the edge of the forest, Kat halted her pony and turned to face the trees. Nikolai and Alexei flanked her.

"What is it?" asked Nikolai.

An invisible horse whinnied in the forest, and another. There was no sign of Sasha.

"Sasha?" whispered Kat. She was afraid of getting no answer.

"There he is!" Nikolai darted his arm up to point Sasha out and groaned as he received a painful reminder from his ribs not to make any sudden movements.

Sasha's pony was walking out of the forest a little way down from where they'd emerged. He seemed in no rush.

"Behind him," said Nikolai, his voice flat. His stomach flipped.

"Oh my God," said Kat. She stood up in her stirrups. "SASHA RIDE... RIDE..."

A line of horseman, extending far to the left and far to the right, appeared at the edge of the forest. They all looked much like the one Kat had seen in the trees, dark hatted, dark coated, dark bearded and all with drawn swords, curved blades that twinkled when they caught the sunlight.

One, directly behind Sasha, stood up in his stirrups, looked down the line to his left, then his right. He raised his sword and yelled.

"Urrraaaaaggghhhh!"

His cry was echoed along the line. Thirty, forty maybe even fifty men roared, waved their swords in the air and spurred their horses forward.

Ahead of them Sasha dug his heels into his pony and it hurried forward. But it was no match for the power of the horses behind him.

"There's no escape," said Nikolai. "This time there really is no escape."

He turned to Kat. "So you were right Katinka, there is no wizard watching over us."

He looked back to the fast approaching horsemen, who were already only a stride or two behind Sasha. "Cossacks," he said. "In the Palace they used to say the Ural Cossacks were the fiercest in all Russia... or was that the Don Cossacks? I can't remember."

Nikolai swallowed. "I hope it's quick, the end I mean." He glanced round at Alexei. "So long, big fellow, it's been nice knowing you – we've had some good times haven't we?"

Alexei was not looking at Nikolai. His attention remained fixed on the charging horsemen. It was, he considered, a magnificent sight. Sergeant Zhukov once told him no man should die without seeing a Cossack charge. He'd spat a wodge of chewed tobacco on to the courtyard floor and added: "Mind you, most men die soon after seeing a Cossack charge at them."

The very earth seemed to shake with the Cossacks' advance, the horses' hooves pounding out a terrible rhythm. Now that he was going to die – Nikolai was right, there really was no escape – Alexei felt himself relax. Life had always been difficult and he wouldn't miss it. Apart from the last few weeks with Kat and Nikolai. He tore his gaze from the Cossacks to his friends. No not his friends, his family. That's what they were. He'd found his family at last and now they were going to die together. Life is cruel, he thought and released one of his giant sighs.

"Why is he smiling?" Kat's voice wobbled a little.

"That's Cossacks for you," answered Nikolai, keen to display his knowledge right to the end, "the most blood-thirsty people in all Russia, aren't they Alexei?"

Alexei grunted his agreement. He'd given up on words entirely – what use had they been to him?

"No, Sasha – look he's smiling."

He was. Beaming actually, standing up in his stirrups, waving his right arm, his dark hair swinging across his forehead. He opened his mouth.

"Urragggghhhh," he roared, matching the Cossacks.

A moment more and he was in front of his sister and her friends. He pulled hard on his reins and the pony stopped at once. It looked at the other ponies, ready to make a complaint. The horses were stopping too. The children were surrounded, horses everywhere, in front of them, behind them and in between them. Kat couldn't see Nikolai or, for once, Alexei.

She was cut off. Except there in front of her was Sasha.

"Our people, sister," he shouted – he had to because the Cossacks were still cheering around them and waving their swords.

"What?"

A Cossack – the one she'd first seen in the forest – appeared alongside Sasha. He stood in his stirrups again, raised his sword high into the sky and roared a command.

"Goodbye, Katinka." Nikolai's voice carried through the men and horses. It sounded like he was about to burst into song (or tears).

There was an eruption of laughter around them, drowning out whatever else Nikolai might have said (in the years to come he steadfastly denied he'd declared his love for Kat).

32

"They found me… it was the Don's son – the Don is the chief. Found me wrapped in a blanket, in a basket with some bread and other sweet foods – an offering you see, for the wood spirits."

They were riding four abreast, Nikolai, Alexei, Kat and Sasha. They'd just waded through a river – "We won't do that again until spring," said Sasha, "it'll be frozen within the week" – and were climbing through another green meadow, the grass so long it brushed their feet (and Alexei's knees) as they rode.

The Cossacks had gone, returned to their daily chores; cooking, cleaning, hunting, sharpening swords, practising sword fighting on horseback, practising riding, practising showing off while riding, standing on one foot on top of the saddle, turning a somersault and landing back in the saddle. Everyday Cossack chores.

Their village was in the next-door valley – through a secret pass that helped keep them out of reach of the Tzar (or Tzarina). The Cossacks of the Hidden Valley were a long-lost legend to most, a spectre St Petersburg mothers used to make their children behave: "If you don't the Cossacks will take you."

But they were real, and they did take Sasha. "They brought me up. I'm part of their family but I always knew I'd come back to Golovina... when I was old enough I'd come home."

"Who left you for the wood spirits?" Nikolai loved a story and this one had him spellbound.

"My father..."

"Your father!"

"My father?" Kat's voice was timid. She was scared. As scared as she'd been at any moment since they'd slipped out of the Winter Palace. She was so close now, so close to home and still nothing made sense, and she wasn't sure she was ready for it to make sense. Sometimes not knowing felt like the best way.

"Yes," said Sasha. He lent across and took her hand. "Our father."

"He came all the way up here from Yegoshikha? To leave you for the wood spirits... why? It doesn't make any..."

"No Katinka, Ivan Dashkov is not my father..."

"So you're not my..."

"He's not your father either."

They'd come to the top of the meadow. It fell away before them until it disappeared into more forest. A little way in front of the trees was a house.

It was large, made of wood and stone and with two turrets. One, on the right, was like the turret of a castle, a secure place in case the house should be attacked. The other was crowned not by battlements but by a blue dome, shaped like an onion and glinting in the sun, which was beginning to take its leave of the day.

"Golovina," said Kat.

"Golovina," said Sasha. "Our home."

A cold wind whispered around them, stirring the grass. The four of them sat on their ponies in silence. The ponies took the chance to chew mouthfuls of grass.

"Our father's home, for a short time our mother's."

Kat closed her eyes. A tear pushed its way out of

her left one. She felt it run down her cheek, over her chin, continue down her neck and dampen her collar. She was home.

"Katinka… we're the same… born with… with, well, what we have…"

He pointed at his top lip. "I was cursed they said. It was Father's family. They said there had to be a sacrifice, the witches and wood spirits had done this, our father and mother must have upset them so… so, I was to be the sacrifice, given to them. Then the curse would be lifted and they could have other children.

"Father took me – I can't remember; I was a baby. Dimitri, the Don's son, he saw – he was out looking for honey. Saw our father, hid and watched. He said our father cried when he laid me down. Cried but never looked back. Dimitri took me home. He's my brother now, my big brother… he's kind of your brother as well. You'll like him…"

"Sasha, Father and Mother… me… what happened…"

"Yes, well – a year or so later you were born. So now they had a hunch-backed daughter and Father's family were not having that, no-one must know they said. The curse is still strong, they said. If anyone finds out we're cursed by the witches and wood spirits we're finished – no-one will have anything to do with us, the townspeople will condemn us, it's a death sentence for all of us…"

"So they got rid of me too?"

"Yes, Mother wouldn't let you be left in the woods so Father paid Ivan Dashkov and his wife to take you… they were childless, desperate for a daughter they told him, would treat you like their own. They were desperate all right, desperate for the money.

"When I found out I swore I'd look out for you and when we were older bring you home… I came to see you, took you into the woods, getting you ready for coming home…"

"I remember," said Kat.

"Then one day I went to Yegoshikha and you weren't there… sold to the Tzar I was told, sold for his circus, my sister…"

Sasha turned in his saddle to look at her. "It killed Mother when she found out, both her children gone, she gave them up without a fight, that's what she believed, so she gave up, died. Father shut the house up and went off to Moscow. Became a soldier… killed in one of Tzar Peter's wars. I swore I'd find you, wherever you were… but there was no need was there? Because you've come home, Katinka."

Kat sniffed. "It's getting dark," she said.

"I'm not afraid of the dark," said Sasha.

"Neither am I," said Kat, "but I want to go home."

She wiped a hand roughly over her face, as if sweeping away the old and letting in the new.

"Race you," she said and dug her heels sharply into her pony's sides. It lurched forward and she wobbled in the saddle. She cackled and set off for Golovina. Sasha made to follow.

"Wait," said Nikolai. "Wait, I want to ask you something…"

"All right," said Sasha, keeping his eyes on his sister's brisk progress down the hill.

"This is Johann Daniel's doing isn't it? He's done this, got us here to you, somehow… with the witches and the wood spirits, whatever they are. He's a wizard himself… but then you know that don't you?"

"I've never heard of him, this French wizard," said Sasha and winked. "Harrghh," he added and his pony needed no further encouragement to hurry after Kat.

Nikolai and Alexei watched him go, Kat a way ahead, nearly at Golovina.

"French… he said French wizard… how did he know he's Fre…"

Alexei raised a mighty hand and brought it down on the rump of Nikolai's pony. So Nikolai never finished his thought, and in all the years he lived at Golovina never found an answer to it either.

The pony leapt in alarm, Nikolai flung his arms around its neck and hung on as the pony set off for home as fast as its little legs could carry it.

Alexei chuckled, gave his pony a gentle squeeze and the unlikely pair, the short, stubby pony and the boy giant, ambled down the hill after the others. Sometimes there were no answers so better not to ask the question. In the distance he watched Kat reach the house, slide off her pony before it had even stopped and hurry to the front door.

"Probably going to count the rooms," said Alexei. He thought that quite a good joke and chuckled again.

Far below he saw the slip of a girl, so light on her feet, push open the front door and step inside. She disappeared from sight.

"Home," he said, out loud again, "Katinka Dashkova is home."

He snorted. "Enough words," he thought, picked up the reins and encouraged the pony to go quicker. He looked up at the snow-covered Urals around them and sucked in the cold air. The blue dome winked at him. Home, they were all home.

Acknowledgements

When you begin to write a book it feels like you're setting off on a lonely journey. By the time you're finished and holding the printed copy in your hand – mouth open in disbelief – it feels like you are part of a team.

Each member of Team Tzar's has played a part in getting this book into your hands. Firstly, I owe an enormous thanks to Mikka and Everything With Words for taking a chance on an unknown, first timer. Without Mikka, Katinka, Alexei and Nikolai would never have made it out into the world. As a wet-behind-the-ears novelist I couldn't have asked for a better editor and publisher. I owe her a great deal. As I do Fritha. Her ideas, guidance, knowledge and support have been invaluable.

Many thanks too to Heather Lacey and Megan – aka the Book Addicted Girl – both Inclusive Minds inclusion ambassadors, who gave up their time to offer perceptive, thoughtful and instructive advice as sensitivity readers. To Sarah, Caroline, Liz, Heidi and all the members of the 'Helensburgh Book and Interiors Club' for their thoughts and encouragement. To Clare Balding for taking the time to be an early reader. To Scott Evans for doing likewise and his generous and persistent championing of the Tzar's.

And to Torrin and Iona who badgered, nagged, hectored and bullied me into trying to write a children's book. This wouldn't have happened without them. Hopefully there will be more for them to read.

Finally, to Karen. She made all this possible.

Q&A with Robin Scott-Elliot

What inspired you to write about a group of children escaping from Peter the Great's Winter Palace?

I love history and I love sport, and that's where the seeds of this story were planted. In the summer of 2012 I was a sports journalist covering the Paralympics and every day across the venues in London I saw amazing people from all around the globe achieve incredible things. It was a life-affirming experience I'll never forget.

When I stumbled across the story of Peter the Great and his Circus of Curiosities, it struck me that to survive in that time and circumstance as a person with a disability you would need to be an incredible person. Almost a superhuman, as the London Paralympians were branded in TV adverts.

It's the steel of Paralympians that formed the basis of the characters of Katinka, Nikolai – who had no name of his own until Kat gives him one – and Alexei.

The Tzar's Curious Runaways has its roots in the traditional adventure story – I love adventure stories – but at its heart it's about Katinka in particular showing the strength, courage and stubbornness not to remain in a role others have defined for her. "I am who I am," she proclaims.

Why did you decide to write a book about Russia?

Russia has always fascinated me. Look at the size of it on the map – it's so big it doesn't fit in one continent. Study the map and each time you'll find a place you've never noticed before that makes you think of adventure, magic and mystery.

Take one example: right over on the east coast there's the Sea of Okhotsk that you just know is full of pirates, giant squid that can swallow a ship whole and an island populated only by exiled children.

I adore history and no country has a bigger, more blood thirsty, jaw-dropping, eyebrow-raising story than Russia. There's the terrible Tzars, there's the Revolution, then there's the millions of Russians who died in the Second World War, the Cold War, the first man in space... the list goes on.

Were Katinka, Alexei and Nikolai real people?

No... and a little bit yes.

In the 18th century if you were an adult or child with a disability, as Katinka, Alexei and Nikolai are in my story, then you were treated differently and more often than not that meant badly.

Tzar Peter collected people with disabilities from around the world as if he was buying a souvenir from his holidays and brought them back to Russia to be part of his Kunstkamera – his 'Circus of Curiosities'. He didn't think there was anything wrong with that, nor did the lords, ladies, soldiers and servants of his court. It seems shocking now but it was accepted then. These 'curiosities' were fed and given a roof over their heads. In return they were mocked, teased, taunted and sometimes worse. That's what happened to Katinka, Nikolai and Alexei.

Thankfully our world is a better place today, although the fight for equal rights and inclusion for all continues.

Are any of the other characters based on real life people?

Yes. History books record that at the court of Peter the Great there was a Garbuchka the Hunchback. And Johann Daniel Schumacher, the cleverest man in Russia, really was Peter's librarian and came all the way from France to serve the Tzar. But he was not a wizard – well, not as far as I know…

You're a sports journalist, used to writing about fast-paced, exciting sporting events – how did this influence your writing in *The Tzar's Curious Runaways*?

There are many ways in which a background in journalism, even sports journalism, can help with longer-form writing.

My favourite form of journalism is the interview because that is discovering and then writing somebody's story. A good interview should become a fine piece of storytelling by the time it makes the newspaper or website.

In journalism, and I think in sports journalism in particular, the pace of the story you are telling is all important and that has a crossover with writing for children – you want to grab attention from the first line and not allow the reader to let go until the final full-stop.

Journalism takes you out into the world, makes you inquisitive as to how the world works, makes you inquisitive how people work, again something I think crosses over with children's literature.

'Why?' you ask again and again, which is just what my children ask me now.